ABOUT THE AUTHOR

Cathryn Hein is the best-selling author of eleven rural romance and romantic adventure novels, a Romance Writers of Australia Romantic Book of the Year finalist with *Santa and the Saddler*, and a regular Australian Romance Reader Awards finalist.

A South Australian country girl by birth, Cathryn loves nothing more than a rugged rural hero who's as good with his heart as he is with his hands, which is probably why she writes them! Her romances are warm and emotional, and feature themes that don't flinch from the tougher side of life but are often happily tempered by the antics of naughty animals. Her aim is to make you smile, sigh, and perhaps sniffle a little, but most of all feel wonderful.

Cathryn currently lives in New South Wales at the base of the Blue Mountains with her partner of many years, Jim. When she's not writing, she plays golf (ineptly), cooks (well), and in football season barracks (rowdily) for her beloved Sydney Swans AFL team.

To discover more about Cathryn and her books, visit cathrynhein.com

Also by Cathryn Hein

Rural Romance
The Country Girl (coming January 2018)
Chrissy and the Burroughs Boy
Wayward Heart
Santa and the Saddler
April's Rainbow
Summer and the Groomsman
The Falls
Rocking Horse Hill
Heartland
Heart of the Valley
The Horseman's Promise

Romantic Adventure
The French Prize

Chrissy *and the* BURROUGHS BOY

CATHRYN HEIN

First published 2017

ISBN 9780648000563

Cover Art by Kellie Dennis at Book Cover by Design
www.bookcoverbydesign.co.uk

For Jim

ONE

AFTER THREE YEARS in a row of being runner-up in the Mount Pitt Australian Rules Football Club's 'best and fairest' award, dislocating a shoulder was not the start to the football season Nick Burroughs had planned. This year was meant to be his.

Instead, halfway through the first quarter of the first game and playing arch rivals the Gerrinton Giants, that oversized peanut Eddie Argyle stuck a boot in Nick's back and launched himself skyward in an attempt to take a screaming mark, only to stuff it up and land the entirety of his great weight directly on Nick. One loud crunch and a roar of pain later, and Nick's best-and-fairest dream was over.

If his shoulder hadn't been so on fire he would have thumped Eddie, but the ignorant lump had galloped off after the ball, leaving Nick on his knees with his teeth jammed together, and his other hand cupping his elbow as he tried to hold his sagging arm in place.

Now, two weeks after the injury, he was propped in the front bar of the Australian Arms Hotel, watching Friday-night footy on the big screen, sipping a beer and brooding over the physio's prognosis.

Another six weeks before he'd be back playing. Half the season gone. Bloody brilliant.

Not.

'You still sulking, Numbnuts?' called his younger brother, Danny, across the bar.

'Piss off,' said Nick.

Danny grinned at the man he was serving. 'Yeah, he's still sulking.'

'It's bad luck,' said Josh Sinclair, who, despite being captain of the Gerrinton Giants, was a top bloke and good footy player. 'You would have been a shoo-in for best and fairest this year.'

'Oi!' said Danny, who was now red-hot favourite. Again. Stuff him. If he and Danny weren't brothers and team-mates, Nick would wish him an injury, too.

Josh laughed and paid for his beer. 'Mate, you're so in love you can barely tie your bootlaces, let alone play decent footy.'

The truth of that, at least, gave Nick some satisfaction. Since meeting his Australian-born, English-raised girl-friend, Beth, last Christmas, Danny had been floating around like one of those dopey cartoon characters with clouds under their feet and love hearts bursting all around their head. Now that Beth had moved permanently to Levenham, where she helped run her grandfather's saddlery, Danny was even worse, hellbent on building a dream life for them both. Footy training was cut short in favour of extra shifts at the pub on top of his regular job of manufacturing and servicing agricultural windmills, so he could afford to buy an even bigger and better love nest than he'd planned. It'd be sickening if the pair of them weren't so happy and mad for each other. Nick was an unsentimental blokey bloke and even he thought them cute.

'What are you doing down here anyway?' Josh asked Nick.

'Chops's girlfriend is over from Warrnambool.'

'Sex in every room,' quipped Danny.

Nick grimaced. 'As long as they're not doing it in mine.'

Josh threw Nick a look of sympathy. 'Stacey here for the whole weekend?'

'Yeah.'

'Bugger.'

Nick shrugged. 'Footy Saturday and we're seeding, so I'm out at the farm anyway.'

'Digby's been flat out at his place, too,' said Josh, referring to his brother-in-law, who had a grazing property and vineyard to the east of Levenham. 'This early rain's been good for everyone. Anyway, I'd best get back to Em before Mum chews her ear off with more parenting advice. I'll catch you boys later.' He grinned. 'I'd wish you luck for tomorrow, but you know how it is. Not that it'd matter. The Giants have this year's premiership in the bag.'

'Yeah, yeah,' said Danny. 'You keep on talking it up, us Pitt boys'll just keep on winning.'

Nick glanced at the telly and sighed. Hawthorn were belting the bejesus out of poor St Kilda and it wasn't even half-time. He checked his watch and made a face. Not yet nine pm and he'd told Chops he'd stay out until ten-thirty. Normally, Nick wouldn't be so generous on the eve of a game, but what did it matter if he turned up at the ground tomorrow a bit tired? He wasn't playing.

Stuff it.

There weren't many occasions when Nick regretted moving from the farm into town, but this was one of them.

He and Charlie Oppenheimer – Chops for short – had been mates since school, and seven months ago sharing a house and a few adventures had seemed like a great idea. As much as Nick adored his family and his mum's cooking, he was twenty-six years old and due some privacy. The rented house meant no worries about bringing a girl home, no one to frown at him if he wandered in a bit under the weather or ate cold pizza for breakfast, and no teenage sister sticking her nose into everything. Just him and Chops, being boys.

Except five minutes in, Chops had ruined it all by finding himself a girlfriend.

Most of the time it was fine. Stacey was studying accounting at the Warrnambool campus of Deakin University and only came home every three weeks or so, with Chops returning the favour when milking allowed. Which was just as well. Nick wasn't sure he could have coped with more of them together. On the weekends Stace was in town Chops was worse than a randy bull, with Stace not much better if the noises Nick had had to endure were any indication.

Tonight wasn't Chops's fault. Nick should have gone to another mate's or the farm rather than the Arms, but with footy on the telly and Danny behind the bar Nick figured he'd have no problems killing a few hours. Instead, he was bored and feeling sorry for himself, his shoulder kept throbbing from the physio's manipulation, and his brother was too busy serving punters to chat for long.

He gazed around for someone to talk to, only to find the crowd was made up of half-cut eighteen-year-olds who made him feel old and grim. Most of the regulars around his own age were upstairs in the pub's private function room at Connor Viccary and Leah Henderson's engagement party. Nick hadn't been invited. No surprise with him being

Leah's ex-boyfriend and Connor harbouring the stupid idea that Nick still had feelings for her, but the bloke always was a peanut.

His brother paused in wiping a spill off the bar to stare at the ceiling, as if worried it might cave in – something he'd been doing all evening. Nick suspected it was more concern about having to deal with drunks from the party later. Connor's mob liked to booze it up.

'You think they'll be a problem?' he asked with a nod upstairs, when Danny came to pick up Nick's empty glass.

'Should be all right. Steve and Barry are up there,' replied Danny, referring to the Arms's burly publican and its bar manager. He lifted Nick's glass and tilted it towards him. 'Want another?'

'Yeah.' After all, Nick had nothing else to do. 'But make it a light.'

He watched football, eking out his beer and trying not to think about his aching shoulder. He hoped Chops and Stacey had worn themselves out. It was going to be hard enough sleeping without their racket adding to his misery.

When Nick could stand it no longer, he slid off his stool, waited to catch Danny's eye, and gave a brief nod of farewell. Danny tossed him a 'you sure?' look that Nick returned with one of his own, communicating that he'd had enough in the wordless way of people who knew each other's quirks instinctively. Danny shrugged a 'suit yourself' and returned to serving.

Careful to protect his shoulder from any accidental bumps, Nick manoeuvred his way through the back of the bar to the rear exit. The barely legal teenagers were getting a bit rowdy but appeared otherwise good-natured. As he passed the wide door to the bistro, he spotted Josh with his wife, Em, relaxing with Josh's parents after their meal. He had his arm slung around Em's shoulders and she was leaning into him, her cheeks flushed with happiness. Josh's mum, Michelle, was rocking a pram back and forth in blissful grandmotherhood, while her husband, Tom, looked on with equal pride.

The sight sent a throb through Nick's chest. Seemed like everyone was in love, except him.

He pushed out into the crisp night and was immediately assaulted by party noise – that raucous, discordant mash of music mixed with people trying to talk over it and each other. Nick wandered further away from the door to peer at the upstairs windows, but the curtains were drawn.

He hoped Leah was having a good time. She was a great girl, pretty and funny, and Nick had liked her a lot, just not in that special forever way. Although it dented his ego, it had been a huge relief to discover Leah felt the same way, and their eventual breakup had been about as amicable as breakups could get. That Leah had found someone to love her properly made Nick glad, even if that someone was Connor Viccary.

The Arms was a corner pub on Levenham's main shopping strip with its own small rear carpark that was well-lit and monitored by several security cameras. Years before, the council had built a large, adjoining carpark, but had run out of funding for lights. Most people parked close to the rear of the main street shops, where there was at least security lighting, but with a waning moon and cloud cover keeping the night dark, and shade trees adding to the shadows, the rest of the asphalted area spread as black as the sky. Not that it bothered Nick. It was early, country town Levenham was hardly a hotspot of violence, and he was more than capable of fending for himself, busted shoulder included. Shoving his hands into his pockets, he stepped out of the halo of light, head down and brooding, the darkness suiting his mood.

Nick was nearing the far side of the carpark when he heard raised voices. He stopped and looked back. A long-legged girl in jeans was hurrying down the strip near the shops, a sloppy-looking bloke on her heels. As she passed a security light, Nick caught a flash of glossy hair and pale, pointed chin and felt a vague tug of recognition. He frowned, trying to place her, then blinked as the bloke who was behind her snatched the girl by the arm and jerked her to a stop. She turned furiously, lifting her arm to tug against his hold, but his grip held.

This didn't look good.

Not letting his narrowed gaze leave either of them, Nick strode quickly back across the carpark.

'Let. Me. Go,' said the girl, gritting out the words.

'Nah, not until you come back inside. You owe me a drink.'

'I told you, I've had enough and I'm going home.'

The girl twisted and yanked hard, but her attacker merely laughed. The hairs on the back of Nick's neck stiffened.

She glanced at the pub only to see the area remained empty. 'Please.' This time there was no grit, only fear.

Her attacker smiled.

Nick broke into a jog.

TWO

NICK SLOWED TO A BRISK WALK, keeping his stride long and his eyes locked on the man in front of him. He recognised the bastard now; Todd Leppington, one of Connor's cronies. He'd been a mean little shit at school and nothing had changed afterwards. Last Nick had heard, Todd was working at the timber mill, where he sat on his arse all day driving a forklift.

Taking advantage of the distraction of Nick's approach, the girl jerked her arm free and stepped backwards. Nick angled towards her and kept his voice casual. 'Everything okay here?'

'Fine,' said Todd, one corner of his lip curled.

'Wasn't asking you.' Nick checked the girl's face and dropped his voice so that she knew how seriously he was taking the situation. 'Are you all right?'

She nodded, although her expression said otherwise. Nick glanced at her hand. Protruding between her fisted fingers was the long, jagged edge of a key.

Pretty and smart. Impressive. He'd have to ask her name when this was over.

'Come on,' he said, 'I'll walk you to your car.'

Todd planted himself in front of them and stabbed a finger at Nick. 'Why don't you mind your own frigging business?'

'Nah, I don't think so.'

'Todd,' said the girl heavily, 'just go back inside.'

Todd's drunken gaze lasered in on her. 'What, now he's here you don't want anything to do with me?'

'Like there's a surprise,' said Nick, unable to help himself.

'Fuck you, Burroughs.'

'I'd rather you didn't. You're not my type.' He touched his hand lightly to the girl's back. 'Let's get you out of here.'

He went to step past Todd, but the peanut blocked his way. Nick suppressed a sigh. He wasn't in the mood for a fight. Todd, on the other hand, seemed to be raring for one. Not that it'd be much of a contest, even with his weak shoulder. Nick was tall and heavily muscled from years of farm work and sport. With his slight beer gut, Todd looked as fit as a pig. Nick had handled calves that were more threatening.

'Don't be a dickhead, Leppo.'

'Who you callin' a dickhead, fuckwit?'

'You. Now get out of the way before I make you.'

The girl shook her head. 'Don't, Nick. He's not worth it.'

'Yeah, right,' said Todd, as if she hadn't spoken. 'I'd like to see you do that with your busted shoulder.'

Nick had had enough. Hands clenched, he stepped towards Todd, gaze like granite. 'It's my left shoulder that's busted. My right fist still works fine.' He took another step. This close, Todd couldn't miss Nick's height and weight advantage. His next words emerged dangerously quiet. 'You want to try it?'

Todd hesitated, then did the smart thing and put his palms up. 'She's all yours, mate.' With a sneer, he began to walk away. 'She's a pricktease, anyway.'

Only the girl grabbing a handful of his shirt stopped Nick from going after him.

'Nick, don't. He really isn't worth it.'

She was right, although that didn't stop him wanting to belt the bastard. He turned back and took proper stock of her. Her blue eyes were wide and her lips were pressed together, and she was rubbing one arm as though cold, but overall she looked fine enough.

'Feeling okay?' he asked. 'Want me to call anyone?'

'No need, I'm good. Thanks.' Then she smiled, and the impact of it was like a cow kick to the chest, stealing Nick of breath and scrambling his brain. This girl wasn't just pretty, she was *gorgeous*.

He grinned back dopily until her fading smile made him realise he was acting like a village idiot. No surprise. Right now, he felt like one.

'So, ah ...' He pointed vaguely towards the line of cars. 'I'll walk you?'

'Sure.'

Nick followed as she stepped out, casting an appreciative gaze over her bum as he probed his soupy brain for who she could be. She wasn't the kind of girl he'd forget in a hurry, yet he was stuffed if he could place her. It was clear she knew him though.

'How did you know my name?'

'Everyone knows the Burroughs boys.'

Nick blinked. This was news. Sure, he'd had his photo

in the paper a few times for footy, but that didn't mean anything.

'They do?'

'Of course.'

'Huh. How 'bout that.'

Suddenly the girl whirled around, causing Nick, who'd been admiring her bum again, to almost crash into her. 'You haven't got a clue who I am, have you?'

He took in her stance: weight on one hip, arms crossed, chin slightly jutted. Trouble. Except the curve of her lips suggested more amusement than anger.

'I feel like I should, but ...' Nick gave a lopsided smile. 'Sorry.'

For a long moment she stared at him, then she huffed out a breath and threw her hands in the air. 'What a waste.'

'A waste?'

'Yeah. A big, fat, gigantic waste.'

Nick gave the back of his neck a scratch. 'Not sure I follow.'

'No, you wouldn't.'

He eyed her warily, the feeling that he'd done something horribly wrong creeping up his belly, which was unfair. He'd saved her from Leppo, done the hero thing. Girls were meant to go for that.

Weren't they?

'I'm Christina James.' She paused, her name hanging, but Nick was clueless. 'Chrissy? From school?'

'Right.'

She tilted her head back to the sky. 'Oh, God, this is too funny.'

It was? Nick was finding it all a bit weird, truth be told. 'Want to fill me in?'

She shook her head again in disbelief. 'You *really* don't remember me?'

'I feel like I do, but I'm buggered if I can figure it out.' He grinned. 'Which is a bit disturbing because there's no way I'd forget someone like you.'

'Someone like me?'

'Yeah.' He shrugged. 'Beautiful.'

She laughed. 'Thanks. A pity you didn't think that seven years ago, but thems the breaks.'

Seven years ago? That meant ...

'We were at school together?'

'Different grade. I was a year below you.'

He frowned. Chrissy was gorgeous. Even with a year's difference he wouldn't have missed her. 'Were you there for only a short time or something?'

'No. I started in Year Eight. Went right through.' She bit the corner of her lip. 'I'll give you a hint: I played netball. Bells ringing yet?'

Netball. He'd always liked netballers. They were sporty, like him, and wore tight lycra uniforms with short skirts that showed off their legs. Two of his girlfriends from back then had been on the school team, and one had even played for Mount Pitt in the league division, which meant he'd watched his fair share of games. Yet he still couldn't place Chrissy.

Nick studied her face. A perfect heart shape with a cutely turned-up nose and clear skin with a sexy flush of pink over her cheeks. She tucked her dark hair behind her ears and angled her head left then right, showing off her profile. Nick rubbed his jaw. Why couldn't he work it out?

She sighed and indicated her perfect white teeth. 'I had braces then. And my hair wasn't like this and I was,' she screwed up her nose and the pink over her cheeks deep-ened, 'a bit overweight.'

Braces, overweight ... Nick's eyes widened. This was chubby Christina? Seriously? A unicorn crossing the carpark farting rainbows couldn't have poleaxed him more.

'Bloody hell.'

'Yep.'

He looked her up and down, gobsmacked. 'You've changed.'

'Not that much.'

'Yes, that much. You're ... you're a babe.'

Chrissy tilted her head and raised a single eyebrow. 'Which made me what, back then?'

Nick swallowed. Any bloke with half a brain could tell this was dangerous territory. 'Ah, young?'

'Very diplomatic. Well done.' She walked on.

Releasing a breath, Nick followed. 'So, what was the big waste you were talking about before?'

She glanced at him sideways without pausing a step. It was a slyly sexy look, but Nick noticed she was still clutching her keys in her fist. He hoped it was because her car was near and not that she had plans on jabbing him.

'Oh, nothing. Just that I had a thumping great crush on you at school and did all sorts of dumb things to get your attention.'

He winced. 'And I never noticed.'

'Nope. Not once.' She threw him another look. 'I thought you might have at least remembered my name though.'

'Sorry.'

'It's okay. It was just school. Life got so much better after that.'

'I dunno. I thought school was fun.'

'You would.'

This time it was his turn to halt. 'What's that supposed to mean?'

'Well, you were Nick Burroughs, weren't you? Just about every girl in school had a thing for you, or your brother.' She began ticking things off her fingers. 'Good-looking, talented sportsman, not completely stupid, nice ... most of the time. Everything was roses for you.'

'But not for you?' He couldn't imagine this beautiful girl not enjoying life. From what he remembered – which wasn't much – Chrissy seemed happy enough then. She'd had friends, and no one had bullied her that he could recall.

'I had plenty of fun times, sure, but when you're a teenage girl and a bit fat and have braces and bad hair, things can get a bit miserable. Especially when the boy you're crushing on doesn't even know you exist.'

'What can I say? I was an idiot.' He bloody was, too. Biggest idiot ever. Then again, maybe it wasn't a bad thing that he hadn't noticed her. Knowing what a peanut he could be back then, Nick probably wouldn't have treated Chrissy right anyway. At least now he was in with a chance.

And he wanted one. Badly.

She laughed. 'Yes, you were. Doesn't matter now. All water under the bridge.' A small white hatchback beeped as Chrissy unlocked it. She paused by the driver's door and smiled at him. 'Thanks for ... you know.'

'You're welcome.' It was time to go, but Nick couldn't make his feet move. She was too pretty, too full of humour and forgiveness. He squinted at the pub and back at Chrissy. 'What was Leppo's problem anyway?'

'I don't know. I was at Leah and Connor's party, and he was in the group I was chatting with. We had a couple of dances, then he bought me a drink and from that seemed to think he was in.'

She crossed her arms and looked down, making Nick wonder how much of a fright she'd had. And if Chrissy was worrying, like he was, about how the situation could have turned out if he hadn't been walking home at the same time. His hand twitched with the urge to touch her, but she dropped her arms and looked up brightly.

'Never mind. Everything's fine now ... thanks to you.'

'I don't know about that. From how you were holding that key, I suspect you would have managed all right without me.'

She held up the key and inspected it. It was a post office box key, long and jagged. 'It might look nasty, but I'm not sure how much damage it would have done.'

'Enough to make Leppo think twice,' he quipped.

'And for me to make a run for it. After I'd kneed him where it hurts, that is. *Hard.*'

'Right.' Nick cringed inwardly at the relish with which she'd said 'hard'. 'Remind me not to get on your bad side.'

They lapsed into silence. Nick racked his brain for something clever and came up blank. By the time it occurred to him to ask how long she was in Levenham for, Chrissy was opening the car door.

'You're on your way home?' she asked.

'Yeah.'

'Can I give you a lift?'

Nick considered. There was nothing more he'd love than to extend his time with her, except his house was so close that getting a lift would only make him look lazy. 'Thanks, but I only live around the corner.'

'I don't mind.'

'It's okay. My housemate's entertaining his girlfriend.'

His mouth twisted wryly. 'The longer I take getting home the better.'

'Ah. Well, thanks.'

'Any time.'

Chrissy nodded and slid into the front seat, flashing a smile when Nick closed the door for her. He stepped back, watching her strap the seatbelt over her chest and lock it in.

With a final small wave, she started the engine and put the car into gear. She was leaving, and Nick was swamped with the horrible idea that he mightn't ever see her again. That whatever goodwill he'd gained by seeing off Todd would be lost by morning.

He couldn't let that happen.

As the car edged out, he tapped the window and made a 'wind down' motion. After a brief hesitation, she obliged.

'What did you do? To get my attention, I mean.'

Chrissy's gaze scanned his face. 'Why?'

He shrugged. 'Curiosity.'

Her eyes never left his face, but her bottom lip was drawn in by the scrape of her top teeth. Seconds passed. Nick tried to keep his expression innocent.

Finally, her gaze shifted to the windscreen and then down. 'You remember the anonymous birthday cards you found in your locker?'

'That was you?'

'Yep.' She gave an embarrassed smile and twisted her hands back and forth around the steering wheel. 'And the Valentine's cards.'

'Jesus.'

'I used to parade up and down in front of you quite a bit, too.' She made a sound like a cut-off laugh. 'You know, in the hope you'd look at me and think, "Jeez, she's hot".'

She looked at him square on then. 'Fat lot of good that did me.'

'What can I say? I was young and stupid.'

'No, you were just you. It was me who was young and stupid. I used to have these jeans that I thought made my bum look skinny. Every casual day I'd wear them and whenever I spotted you I'd do this special walk, one that made my bum wiggle. You know what happened?'

He shook his head.

'The school nurse took me aside and asked if I had a problem downstairs that I needed to talk to someone about.' Chrissy put her palms to her cheeks, fingers covering her eyes. 'I could have died.'

'I bet,' he said, his expression pained. That must have been horrible.

She splayed her fingers and looked through the gaps at him. 'There's more.'

'More?' Bloody hell.

She pushed her fingers together and nodded. 'Notes tucked into your football kit.'

Nick remembered those. 'They were sweet.'

'That time when I bought every one of your raffle tickets?'

'Hang on, weren't they for your parents?'

'No. I bought them, just so I could stand near you and breathe the same air for a while.' She dropped her hands to her lap. 'Remember the phone calls? The ones where some girl would call and then say nothing?'

Okay, so they weren't so sweet. They were weird. Except for one time.

'*I just needed to hear your voice,*' said Nick, recalling her words. He'd puzzled over that for weeks, eavesdropping in on conversations, but he'd never recognised the voice.

'That was me. Teenage crushes suck.'

'They sure do.' He curled his hand around the edge of the window. 'I'm going to make up for it though.'

'Oh yeah? How?'

'You'll see.' Nick straightened and grinned down at her. 'I'll see you around.'

She laughed and this time when she drove away he didn't stop her.

It wasn't until he was striding across the carpark that Nick realised his mistake and could have thumped himself. Not only did he not know if Chrissy was single, she probably didn't even live here, 'cause he sure would have noticed if she did.

Which was going to make atoning for his adolescent stupidity pretty difficult.

Bloody peanut.

THREE

CHRISSY REGARDED the macadamia-nut slice Kai had slid in front of her. As with everything else the chef made, it looked mouth-watering. The base appeared biscuity and sweet, its thick centre a dark gold and laden with nuts, the chocolate top finished to a mirror shine.

'Seriously, Kai, you have to stop.'

At the mention of 'stop' the chef stiffened, lifted his nose and puckered his mouth. 'And that would be why?'

'Because I'm going to end up enormous, that's why.'

'But you adore my cooking.'

'Yes. That's why I'm going to end up enormous if you keep bringing me things. I can't resist.'

'But my little truffle,' said Kai, putting on an over-the-top French accent, 'it is only a *petit* piece.' He squeezed his thumb and forefinger together for emphasis.

Chrissy regarded the plate and arched an eyebrow.

The chef merely blinked his innocence and gave a Gallic shrug, before reverting to his usual broad Australian accent. 'There's not that much sugar, and nuts are good for you. Besides, you need to keep your energy up.'

'I can do that with a banana.'

'Ah,' he said, leaning across her desk, his soft brown eyes sparkling, 'but where's the fun in that? Bananas are boring. Pretty girls like you deserve caramel and chocolate.'

Although she was laughing inside, Chrissy remained sober. 'You do realise that all this flattery and bribery won't influence the newsletter layout.'

Kai reared back and slapped a hand to his barrel chest. He was a big man, edging towards overweight, but his height meant he carried the excess better than most. He was attractive, too, in an aging salt-and-pepper way. 'How could you think such a thing? The Kitchen Kaiser possesses no ulterior motives.' The Kitchen Kaiser being a nickname afforded Kai by the local *Levenham Leader* newspaper after Ryan's Winery Restaurant received a rave review in a prestigious national food magazine, amusing Ryan's small team of staff no end. Kai had since adopted the title with glee.

'Is that so?'

'Of course. Although, if you could allocate a soupçon more copy to the restaurant.' He batted his lashes.

Chrissy's laughter finally broke. He was the funniest man. 'Go rule your kitchen, Kaiser. I have work to do.'

'Don't forget to eat your slice.'

'I won't. And Kai?' She smiled when he turned. 'Thanks for being such a sweetheart.'

He nodded, serious for once. 'It can be hard, starting a new job. I just wanted to make you feel welcome.'

'You have. Everyone has.'

Chrissy glanced around her small, timber-panelled office on the mezzanine floor above the winery's cellar-door sales room, her gaze lingering on the large panoramic photo of Ryan's Winery hanging on the wall. The scene encompassed the entire complex — the architect-designed stone cellar door and its adjoining restaurant, the winery with its crush and vats, and the expansive gardens that, although young, were so lovely they were destined to become an attraction in themselves.

In the centre of the photograph the Ryan family formed a relaxed group. Alistair, the founder, stood with his hand rested on the shoulder of his garden-mad wife, Yvette, both smiling proudly at the camera. Their son, Shaun, now chief winemaker, stood alongside with his beloved grey Irish wolfhound, Shamrock, at his feet. They made an attractive, if small family, but what drew the eye was their pride. What had started out as a hobby in a non-winegrowing area was now a success that had sparked others to follow, and created a new and exciting wine region with a unique terroir.

'I just hope I do them justice.'

'You will. You have passion, like me.' Kai nodded at the plate. 'Now eat.'

As the chef departed, Chrissy stared again at the photograph and experienced another knot of nerves. She wanted this job to work out, not just for the Ryans but for herself. Her position as marketing and customer service manager posed enormous challenges and opportunities. Although she'd be working very closely with the Ryans, the role was Chrissy's to develop however she thought best, and the perfect chance to prove herself. Compared to similar family-owned wineries in established regions, Ryan's production was small, but Levenham's singular terroir and Shaun's oenological skills made their wines special.

There'd be no corporate ladder like her last position, probably no overseas travel, but this was a winegrowing district on the rise and a winery crafting wines that surprised even the most cynical critic. With more of the original farmland earmarked for expansion and new vines scheduled to come into production over the next few years, the potential for market growth was huge. She'd have autonomy, a challenge. The future was bright.

And it was home.

Kai was right. She did have passion, oodles of it, and Chrissy was determined that it would shine through in everything she did.

She regarded the photograph again and winked, then picked up her caramel slice, took a large bite and knuckled down to work.

———

'You shouldn't have left so early on Friday night,' said Chrissy's friend and North Levenham Rebels teammate Alice Lindner as she passed the netball. For a sweet-faced elfin girl who looked a lot like her animated Wonderland namesake, Alice could throw hard and fast. She'd been working at her family's garden centre in one form or another all her life, and it had left her surprisingly strong.

Chrissy caught the ball easily and speared it straight at her other friend Paige de Bruin, who, thanks to her Dutch heritage, was the exact opposite to Alice and built like an Amazon. Coupled with her keen librarian's mind, she could be an intimidating woman, but Paige's heart was as big as the rest of her and Chrissy adored her.

Chrissy's passes weren't as sharp as they'd once been, but that was understandable given she hadn't played since leaving university. Rejoining her old netball team was another thing to add to her growing list of wonderful things to return home to. She missed the camaraderie, competition and community spirit of team sport, and working out in a gym didn't compare. Netball was exercise made fun.

'Don't tell me,' she said, 'Connor got naked.'

'Eww,' said Paige, who happened to be Connor Viccary's cousin.

'Thankfully, no,' said Alice, catching Paige's pass and throwing the ball straight to Chrissy. She paused to retie her long blonde ponytail, talking around the hairband gripped between her teeth. 'But I'm pretty sure Makenna Josling did with Liam O'Donnell after.'

Chrissy nearly dropped the catch. 'Seriously?'

Alice nodded, her eyes bright with merriment.

'Wow.'

'I know!'

'I hope she used protection,' said Paige. 'Who knows where Liam's bunged his bratwurst.'

The girls collectively screwed up their noses at the thought. Liam O'Donnell might be good-looking, but he had a reputation, and it wasn't nice.

They continued with their warm-up, readying for practice on number three court at Wallace Park, the town's netball and tennis complex. Being Tuesday night, their arch rivals the South Levenham Saints had the main court and the pleasure of its new all-weather acrylic coating. Thursday would be the Rebels' turn. Funding for more resurfacing was in the pipeline, or so the government had promised, but country towns like Levenham had never been much of a priority.

'Hey,' said Chrissy, bulleting another pass and feeling pleased with her improving power. 'Guess who I bumped into in the carpark after.'

'Who?'

'Nick Burroughs.'

Alice caught the ball and held it, her gaze turning dreamy. 'I wish he'd bump into me. That man is such a hottie.'

'Brother's better,' said Paige. 'Total babe.'

'Is not!' exclaimed Alice, looking outraged at the claim. Until she'd started going out with Eddie Argyle in Year Twelve, Alice's teenage crush on Nick had been nearly as bad as Chrissy's.

'Danny's off the market now anyway,' said Paige. 'So, what happened with Nick?'

'Nothing much.' Chrissy kept her tone nonchalant. 'Todd was being an idiot. Nick stepped in.'

Paige narrowed her eyes. 'What do you mean, Todd was being an idiot?'

'He followed me out, carrying on about how I couldn't leave because I owed him a drink. Grabbed my arm.'

'What a turd,' said Alice.

'I'll tell Connor,' said Paige. 'He'll have a word.'

'Don't bother. It was no big deal.'

Paige didn't look like she believed Chrissy, which didn't surprise her. Paige had firsthand experience of men who thought they could treat women however they liked.

'What did Nick do?' asked Alice.

'Stood over him and scared him off. Todd was being all smart about some injury Nick had and Nick said that it was only his shoulder that was busted not his fist, and did Todd want to test it out.' She grinned at the memory. 'It was pretty cool.'

Although 'cool' wasn't the right word. Nick's heroics had been hot, as her fantasies had been reminding her nonstop these past four days.

Alice sighed. 'I bet it was.'

'Then what happened?' asked Paige.

'Nothing much.'

'What? Nick just walked away? Come on.'

Chrissy spun the ball on her finger as she considered how to explain the strange combination of frustration, embarrassment and excitement that had been 'afterwards'.

'He walked me to my car.'

'Oh,' breathed Alice. 'How gentlemanly.'

'Yeah.' Chrissy bounced the ball once and fired it at Alice. 'I thought so, too until I realised he had no idea who I was.'

Both girls boggled their eyes at her.

'But ...' Alice's mouth popped like a goldfish. 'You've loved him, like, *forever.*'

'Not *forever.* I had a crush on him at school, that's all.' A pretty major one, admittedly, but a crush isn't love and her feelings had soon faded once Chrissy had left town for university. Well, dulled, mostly.

'Surely he must have remembered you though?' asked Paige.

'Nope. I had to tell him who I was, and even then he was like, "Who?" Can you believe that? After all the embarrassing things I used to do.' Chrissy stared at her feet for a moment, shaking her head. 'I was so shocked I started to laugh at the irony of it and he was all, "What?" So, I told him about my crush and parading up and down in front of him wiggling my bum like a prize parrot. I even admitted it was me that left the notes and cards.'

Alice's jaw dropped so wide you could have popped a tennis ball in her mouth. 'You did?'

'As embarrassing as it was, I did. Anyway, it was school. We all did dumb stuff then. None of it matters now.' She gave a sniff. 'I certainly don't care.'

Paige shared a sly look with Alice. 'What did he say when you told him all that?'

'Not much.' Chrissy shrugged. 'Just that he was an idiot and he was sorry.'

'Aww,' said Alice, smiling, 'that's so sweet.'

Chrissy held out her hands for a pass, but it never came. Paige had the ball balanced on her hip and was watching Chrissy closely. 'Anything else?'

There was plenty. Most of it was the way Nick had looked at her, as though she was the most amazing girl he'd ever seen. It had made Chrissy's stomach flutter and her heart gallop, but that didn't mean she trusted it. His sudden attraction seemed a hell of an about-face, especially after so many years of being ignored.

'He said he was going to make it up to me.'

'Make it ...' Alice slapped her hands to her cheeks and did a little jig. 'Omigod!'

'Settle, petal,' said Chrissy, rolling her eyes. 'It's not like he meant it.'

'Of course he meant it! Look at you.' Alice waved her arm up and down, indicating Chrissy's face and body. 'How could he not?'

'Exactly,' said Paige. 'You're babelicious and he's single. Trust me, he meant it.'

Alice nodded. 'Single and a total hottie.'

'Sporty, too.'

'Local farm boy – they're always adorable. It's the animals, looking after them. Teaches them patience and compassion. Even Eddie was—' Alice clamped her mouth shut. Eddie was a no-go zone. 'Anyway, farm boys are lovely.'

Paige twirled the netball. 'Nice family. His mum's a darling.'

Over her momentary Eddie-lapse, Alice continued to nod like a bobble toy. 'Decent people, the Burroughs.'

Chrissy folded her arms and lifted her eyes heavenwards.

Paige simply laughed and winked. 'Fantastic kisser.'

'You've kissed him?' asked a wide-eyed Alice. 'When?'

'Not me! Leah. She went out with him for ages, remember?' Paige tossed the ball to Alice. 'She said he was ama-a-a-zing.'

Alice cuddled the ball to her belly and sighed. 'Why doesn't that surprise me? You only have to look at him to know those lips would make your toes curl.' Suddenly she speared the ball at Chrissy. 'You need to take one for the team and go there.'

'No, I don't.'

'You do,' agreed Paige.

'Yeah? Okay then, if Nick was so *amazing*, why did he and Leah break up?'

'Because there was no real spark between them,' said Paige. 'Even Leah admitted that.'

'And as we all know,' said Alice, 'a girl doesn't just need sparks. She needs fireworks. Which is why you,' she cocked a finger at Chrissy, 'need to do the team thing and get it on with Nick. I bet the two of you would go off like rockets.'

'No.'

'Why not?' asked Alice. 'You're home for good now.'

'Because I'm *busy*.'

'Doing what?'

Chrissy blinked at her, then huffed out a breath. 'Oh, not much. Just settling in to my new job, unpacking, sorting myself out after ... You know.'

Paige waved that away. 'Forget Owen. He's long gone.'

'And he was a cheating bastard.'

'He was,' admitted Chrissy, 'but he was also my boyfriend for nearly a year.'

And a good part of the reason she'd gone hunting for a new job. Owen had worked at the same city-based wine conglomerate, albeit in a different department, and contact between them was unavoidable, which wouldn't have been so bad if Chrissy hadn't also had to deal with the girl he'd slept with. The truth was Chrissy hadn't been enjoying the work anyway. It was too removed from what she really loved, which was the vineyards and wineries, and the people who worked them. Spotting the Ryan's Winery advertisement barely a few weeks after the breakup had been a godsend in more ways than one.

'Yeah, so?' scoffed Paige, folding her arms and mirroring Chrissy. 'What? You still love him?'

'No!'

Paige shrugged a shoulder. 'There you go. Time to get back in the saddle.'

'Or on it,' said Alice. 'Which would be no hardship with Nick.'

'I don't know. I reckon Nick could get pretty hard.'

The pair looked at each other straight-faced, then cracked up.

'Sorry to disappoint you matchmakers,' said Chrissy, as their coach blew her whistle and waved the team over, 'but you'll have to live vicariously through someone else. The only thing I have time for is my new job.'

'And us,' said Alice, slinging an arm over her shoulder, while Paige joined the hug from the other side.

Chrissy laughed. 'And you two.'

FOUR

NICK CHECKED himself out in the wardrobe mirror of his old bedroom at the farm and grimaced. It was his mum's fiftieth birthday and the extended Burroughs clan was invading Ryan's Winery to celebrate. To save himself a drive back into town, Nick had showered and changed at the farm.

He'd spent most of the afternoon on the tractor, seeding forage oats that they'd strip-graze throughout the winter and bale for hay in the spring, which had left ample time for his mum to spot the clothes he'd tossed on his old bed that morning. Now, thanks to her precision ironing, he looked exactly like he used to – like a bloke who lived at home and let his mum do everything.

Not the image he was after, but any attempt at rumpling and his mum would clip his ear, and he wasn't about to upset her on her birthday.

'Numbnuts!' yelled his sister, Ebony, as she barged in without knocking.

Numbnuts. Jesus, now his sister was calling him that. Good one, Danny. Bloody peanut.

He regarded her with big-brother sternness. 'Don't let Mum hear you calling me that or there'll be trouble. Nice frock, by the way.'

Ebs threw him a teenage sneer and continued bouncing from foot to foot with her arms behind her back.

He suppressed a sigh. 'Okay, what?'

'Mum says you have to wear a tie!'

'Don't have one.'

Ebony thrust a hand forward. 'That's okay. Mum says you can wear one of Dad's.'

Nick looked at the tie dangling from her fist. It was brown. Brown and sort of shiny, and very, very broad. 'Nah.' He swiped his hands down the front of his shirt and winked. 'I look swish enough without it.'

'But you *have to*!' His little sister bugged her eyes at him. At thirteen, she was a fireball of horse-mad energy and mischief and Nick adored her. The entire Burroughs clan did. She was 'the accident', a happy but late addition to the family when everyone, including his parents, had thought Danny and Nick would be it.

Ebs could also be a complete pain in the arse when the mood took her.

He went to ruffle her hair and thought better of it. For once, Ebony's hair was clean and combed. Mum had probably spent an age trying to get it neat. 'Good try, squirt.'

'Aw.' Ebony's shoulders sagged. Playing tricks on her brothers had been a favourite pastime, but with both of them now moved out of home, there was only Mum and Dad, and they weren't nearly as much fun.

'Yeah, yeah. I'm a spoilsport. But you gotta remember, I've been around a lot longer than you. Where'd you get it from anyway?'

'Grandpop's box.'

'Figures. Now go put it back and try not to get dirty while you're at it.'

He watched her stomp off and smiled. Ebs was still a little girl, but she was growing up fast, and though a rabid tomboy right now, there'd come a time when the local lads would start sniffing around. Probably sooner rather than later, given Ebony's prettiness and bouncy-bright personality. Nick wasn't sure how any of them would cope. The thought of anyone even looking at his little sister sideways made him want to thump something. He couldn't begin to imagine how his dad felt.

'Ebony!' His mother's voice echoed up the hall from the kitchen. 'What did I tell you?'

Nick shook his head. Ebs must have dirtied her dress, which meant it'd be smart to avoid the kitchen for a few minutes in case war broke out. Shooting a last glance at the mirror to check his shirt was tucked in properly, he wandered to the lounge, sank into a chair and flicked the television to the football channel. A panel was discussing the weekend's upcoming games. Nick tried to concentrate, needing the intel for his weekend footy tips, but within moments he was back to daydreaming about Chrissy James.

Five days had passed since he'd bumped into her in the carpark and Nick had thought about her on every one of them. He still couldn't believe he hadn't noticed her at school. Even overweight and with braces there must have been some hint of the girl she'd grow into, but nup, his peanut brain had missed it completely. Not that he was alone there. No one else in his group had paid Chrissy James any attention either. Except they hadn't been on the receiving end of those notes and cards and phone calls.

Nick slid his phone from his pocket and checked Ryan's website again. Chrissy's blue eyes smiled out at him from her staff photo, causing his heart to thump. Not only was she gorgeous, she was smart, with a degree in marketing and an impressive-sounding job title.

Most of all, she was here.

It hadn't taken much to discover where she was working. When he'd quizzed them on Saturday morning, Chops and Stacey had had no idea, so Nick had asked Danny, who, thanks to his job at the Arms, knew pretty much everyone. His brother had the answer in minutes – after a stint working interstate, Chrissy had recently joined the staff of Ryan's Winery. News so good Nick would have put Danny in a headlock and knuckled his brother's skull in affection and appreciation if they'd been chatting in person.

Pity it was the cellar door she ran and not the restaurant, or he'd be able to start his seduction tonight. Then again, given the embarrassing knife-sharp creases down the legs of his chinos and sleeves of his shirt, and the gathering of nosy relatives who loved nothing better than a budding romance to gossip about, it was probably a good thing Chrissy wouldn't be there. They'd only scare her off and Nick didn't want Chrissy going anywhere other than into his arms.

Bed would be nice, too, but he had a whole lot of ground to make up before that chicken hatched.

It was another fifteen minutes before they were ready to leave. Seeing her dressed up and looking gorgeous, Nick kissed his mum. Three kids and a lifetime of hard work helping run the farm and she still looked great.

'Looking pretty glam there for an old girl,' he teased.

It was true. Judy didn't dress up often, but when she did it reminded them all what a beauty she was. Her shoulder-length dark hair curled softly around a face made more attractive with dashes of mascara, blush and lipstick. A fitted blue-and-black print dress showed off her curvy figure, while high heels made her shapely legs appear even longer. Both his parents were tall and good-looking, traits their offspring had inherited, although Ebs still looked like a gangly foal.

'Who are you calling an old girl?' She tugged his ear playfully. 'I'm still young enough to keep you in line.'

Nick's dad walked into the room, expression suspiciously smug. Pausing a short distance from his wife, he looked her up and down and rubbed his chin. 'Think that dress needs something.'

Sensing drama, a wide-eyed Ebs tucked her hands under her armpits and wriggled.

Judy smoothed the sides of her dress. 'What's wrong with it?'

Suddenly, the kitchen bristled with tension. Nick glared at his dad, who carried on as though unaware of the change.

'Nothing. You look as beautiful as always.' He stepped closer, dug into his pocket and held out a closed fist. 'I just thought it'd look better with this.' Grinning, Nick's dad slowly opened his fingers.

Judy's fingers flew to her mouth. 'Oh.' She blinked rapidly. 'Oh, Steven.'

It was a necklace and pendant. She held it up and inspected it, and her eyes turned even more liquid. Nick and Ebs snuck closer for a look.

The pendant was round and segmented, a central disc surrounded by four concentric rings, all made of gold. But what had choked Judy up were the engravings. Her name was etched in the central disc, followed by Ebony's on the first ring, then Danny's, Nick's and finally Steve's on the outer ring.

The Burroughs family, orbiting the woman they adored and who made them whole.

It was perfect. Nick cast his dad an approving nod, but Steve was too busy thumbing a tear from his wife's cheek.

He cupped her neck and kissed her. 'Shall I put it on for you?'

She nodded vigorously, then, noticing her children, feigned a scowl. 'Did you two know about this?'

Nick and Ebs shook their heads. As his dad fitted the necklace, Nick guided his sister aside to give his parents space to enjoy the moment, and watched them with a kind of awe.

Any number of times throughout the years, his dad had surprised them with his romantic gestures. His father might be a daggy farmer most of the time, but when it came to his wife, he knew how to be a man. Nick and Danny had discussed it one night, when they'd had too many beers and were feeling sulky over their single statuses. Both had agreed that if they had a chance at the sort of love their parents shared, they'd shift heaven and earth to make it happen. Danny had recently succeeded with Beth. Nick was still searching.

Although maybe, just maybe, that search might finally be over.

———

Someone had taken a lot of trouble to decorate the Burroughs' tables. Each had a bouquet of golden helium-filled balloons as its centrepiece. Tiny gold fives and zeroes were scattered over the white tablecloth and gold ribbon had been used to tie the napkins. Even the steel ice buckets had white towels with gold edges draped over their bottles of sparkling wine.

'Did you organise this?' Nick asked his dad as they stood near the entrance, greeting guests.

'Nope. Restaurant did it all. Did a good job, too. Your mum looks happy.'

'Nice work with the necklace.'

'I thought so.' Steve regarded his wife, who was trying to deal with yet another armful of flowers. 'She deserves it.' He left to relieve her of her burden.

His dad's place was immediately filled by Danny and Beth, who had her hair up in a messy kind of bun and was looking ridiculously pretty in a pale-yellow dress. It was autumn in Levenham, but between her dress, cute freckles and bright smile, Beth was pure summer sunshine. No wonder his brother was crazy about her.

Nick kissed her check and, lowering his voice yet keeping it loud enough for Danny to hear, murmured, 'You're looking too good for him, as usual. One of these days you'll realise you chose the wrong brother.'

'Piss off, Numbnuts,' said Danny, without rancour. Nick's teasing of Beth about her choice was a running joke that no one took seriously. 'Shit, the grannies are here.' He reached out his hand for Beth's. 'Quick, before they spot us.'

'What's your problem?' asked Nick. Danny normally adored his grandmothers.

'Them.'

Nick shot a puzzled glance at Beth.

'Don't look at me.' She pointed at Danny. 'It's him that's scared.'

'Too right I am,' said Danny, eyeing his approaching grandmothers, who looked as sprightly as ever, if a little narrow-eyed with determination as they spotted their grandsons. The two women had been friends for years and liked to attack as a pair.

'Weddings,' said Beth in explanation.

'Rabid with it.'

Of course the grannies were. Everyone was hanging out for news of Danny and Beth's engagement. The Burroughs clan loved a celebration, but weddings were a particular favourite.

'Yeah?' said Nick. 'And?'

'Give us a break. We've only just moved in together.'

Beth leaned against Danny and squeezed his hand. 'I can handle it.'

'I know, baby. But it's getting ridiculous.' He side-stepped towards the bar. 'Drink?'

'Sook,' said Nick.

'You wait till it's your turn and see how you like it. Anyway, has to be me doing the bar run.' He used his chin to indicate Nick's shoulder. 'You can't carry anything.'

Which wasn't quite true. Nick could, it just hurt if he got the angle wrong. He rubbed a hand through his hair and sighed. Without Danny or Beth, the grannies would zero in on Nick and his lack of love-life, which was Danny's plan, of course, but Nick supposed they could do with a break. 'Make it quick. Man's not a camel, you know.'

'It's about time you found yourself a nice girl like your brother,' said Nanna Burroughs once the cheek kissing and niceties were over.

'Nah, happy playing the field.' He winked naughtily at her. 'More fun that way.'

'Fun?' said Granny Yates. 'From what I hear the only fields you've been playing lately are the farm's.' She tapped his chest. 'You're too picky, that's your trouble.'

Nanna Burroughs nodded in agreement. 'If you're not careful all the good ones will end up taken.'

Feeling desperate, Nick searched the bar for Danny, relieved when he spotted him with his hands loaded, but still too far away.

Fortunately, Beth came to the rescue, distracting the grannies with more hellos and cheek kissing, followed by a question about whether they were coming to the football game on Saturday. Which immediately fired an animated discussion about Mount Pitt's chances for the premiership this year. Nick could have kissed her. Instead, he snatched a beer from his brother and took a gulp.

'You took your time,' he muttered.

Danny regarded him without pity. 'Not fun, is it?'

Nick didn't reply. He was too busy fixing his gaze on the shapely woman backing out through the kitchen's swinging doors. Then she turned and Nick nearly choked.

What the hell was Chrissy doing here?

Not just here, but waitressing. And on his mum's party night with all his family present and, God help him, the grannies, and when Nick was looking like a dork thanks to his mum's ironing.

Feeling Danny's gaze, Nick quickly looked away and feigned interest in his beer, but that lasted all of five seconds. His eyeballs tracked back to Chrissy as though attached by elastic.

She flowed between groups, offering nibbles from her tray with expert grace and passing napkins with a kissable pink-lipsticked smile. She was wearing a cream-coloured blouse made of some sort of thin shiny fabric that floated over her breasts like a caress. Her skirt was fitted too, curving around her hips and bum so perfectly that just looking at it made Nick's brain blank out.

Beth tugged on his sleeve. 'Earth to Nick.'

'What?'

She exchanged a look with Danny, who was clearly finding the whole thing highly entertaining. To everyone's relief, the grannies had moved on to other prey.

Nick's eyes narrowed. 'Did you know she'd be here?'

Danny shook his head. 'Nope.'

'You sure?'

'Yeah, I'm sure. As far I as I know, she works for the winery.'

Which is what the website staff profile had said too, yet here she was looking stunning while Nick was at his self-conscious worst and, even more awkward, surrounded by his boisterous, sticky-beaking family.

As though sensing their attention, Chrissy shifted her head from the group she was serving and locked eyes with Nick. For a few intense moments she simply stared, then her mouth curved and her blue eyes shone, and her cheeks flushed so prettily it was like watching the first bloom of sunrise spread across the sky, except even more breathtaking.

The room noise fell away until all Nick was left with was the sound of his heart as it tumbled over and over itself before giving a last vertigo-inducing lurch and landing with a loud splat into a big squishy pile of love.

FIVE

NICK TRACED the line of her jaw and throat with his gaze as Chrissy leaned to place his plate on the table in front of him. A waft of something deliciously sweet, like apricots, surrounded him, making him feel even more drugged than he already was. His eyes dipped to her chest, where her shirt gaped slightly, and caught a hint of white lace.

He swallowed and found his voice. 'Thanks.'

'You're welcome.' Chrissy's smile immediately transferred to Beth, who was sitting alongside him. 'I won't be a minute.'

Nick's eyes followed her to the kitchen and stayed on the door until she reappeared carrying more plates.

'Enjoy,' Chrissy said to Beth and went to move on.

Nick couldn't stand it. Chrissy had been so busy serving all they'd had time for was a quick hello. He touched her arm, desperate to talk. 'What time do you—'

'Sorry, Nick, I really have to get these meals out.'

Disappointment sat heavy in his belly. He stared at his steak, not wanting it. Then he breathed in and forced himself to concentrate on his meal, but could feel Beth eyeing him sideways.

'You like her,' she said.

'Who?'

'Don't try to fob me off, Nick, or I'll tell the grannies.'

Overhearing 'grannies', Danny, who was next to Beth and had been chatting with his Uncle Des, immediately butted in. 'What about the grannies?'

Beth raised her eyebrow slightly.

'Nothing,' muttered Nick.

'Just whether Nick or I would give them a lift to football on Saturday,' said Beth smoothly.

'Let Numbnuts do it. You have enough with the shop.' Problem solved, Danny turned back to his uncle, leaving Nick at Beth's mercy again.

'So, who is she?'

'Just a girl from school.'

'Just a girl from school.' Beth nodded to herself. 'Why does she keep looking at you, then?'

Nick's gaze shot up. Chrissy was moving around the corner of the table, topping up water glasses, her focus on everything but him.

Beth grinned.

'Yeah, funny.'

'I thought so.' She contemplated Chrissy as she chewed. 'She's very pretty.'

Nick said nothing.

'The question is, what are you going to do about it?'

'About what?'

'*Grannies.*'

Nick readjusted his thoughts on his brother's girlfriend. She wasn't bright and sunny at all. She was a dark-hearted witch.

A smile tilted her lips. 'I thought the legend was that when you Burroughs boys spotted the girl of your dreams you just went for it. Danny did.'

His brother had too. The odds of Danny winning Beth's heart had been remote, especially when he'd learned she was only in Levenham to help out in her grandfather's saddlery over Christmas, but he'd won her love anyway. If his brother could do it, then Nick sure as shit could. Except unlike Nick and Chrissy, Danny and Beth had had no high school history messing things up.

'Don't think that'll work,' he said.

'Really?'

'Yeah, really.'

'Why?'

Nick contemplated the slice of steak he'd just cut and set down his fork. He searched nearby, checking whether Chrissy was within hearing distance, but she was across at his parents' table, one hand behind her back as she expertly poured wine. Maybe Beth would be able to help.

'Story is she had a big crush on me at school, did all this embarrassing stuff to get my attention and I never noticed.'

Beth glanced at Chrissy and then stared at Nick like he was the world's biggest tool. 'You're joking, aren't you?'

'Nope.'

'But ...' She glanced at Chrissy again and frowned. 'How?'

Wasn't that the million-dollar question. What could he say? That back then she was overweight and had braces and he was too shallow and up himself to bother looking deeper? Yeah, like that'd go down well.

Unable to help himself, Nick ran another appreciative look over her much-altered body. That skirt and top were seriously sexy. No panty line that he could see, which meant maybe ...

Beth clicked her fingers in front of his face.

Nick grinned and picked up his fork. 'Sorry.'

'You were saying?'

He blinked. What had he been saying? Oh yeah. Nick took his time to chew and swallow before answering. 'She was different back then.'

'How different?'

Lowering his chin, Nick fixed on his plate and mumbled something that sounded like, 'Bit tubby.'

Beth cupped a hand around her ear and leaned close. 'What was that? Did I just hear you say she was a bit—'

'Shh!' Nick shot a panicked look around the table. Nobody seemed to be listening in, but you could never be too sure with his nosy family. Beth was shaking her head. He sneered back. 'Go on, say it. You're dying to.'

'Okay, I will. No wonder you're single. You're an idiot.'

'Bit harsh.' He cut into a crunchy green bean. 'I've grown up since then.'

'Hmm,' said Beth.

'Have.'

Beth raised an eyebrow.

'I have! Anyway, I'm going to make it up to her.'

'Are you now. How?'

Good question.

He took a sip of wine, watching Chrissy over the rim of his glass as she reached past a cousin to retrieve an empty bottle off the table. 'No idea, but I'll think of something.'

He was a Burroughs boy who just might have found his special forever girl. There was only one way ahead: he would win her over or humiliate himself in the process.

Humiliate ... Now there was an idea. A bloody uncomfortable one, but maybe worth it.

Nick cast another look at Chrissy. Oh yeah, definitely worth it.

———

Nick leaned against the front of his ute with his arms and legs folded, and tipped back his head to scan the sky for the Southern Cross. The night was clear and he found the constellation's four points and offset fifth star easily. He smiled, feeling lucky, and resumed his vigil on the restaurant door.

Chrissy's car was parked in the far corner, near the winery offices. He'd spotted it on leaving and, shunting Ebs off with his mum and dad, had feigned mucking around on his phone while the rest of the Burroughs clan had made their noisy departures. A few lingered in the carpark, throwing him curious looks as they rounded off unfinished conversations. Danny and Beth had hung around for a few words, before Danny had wrapped his arm around Beth's shoulders and whispered in her ear. Beth had turned pink and allowed herself to be dragged off, but not before sneaking a wink at Nick and mouthing 'good luck'.

And there he was thinking he'd been subtle.

Light flashed as the restaurant door opened. Nick straightened, his breath shortening as he watched the silhouetted figure pause for a moment before letting the door shut.

'Thought I'd hang around and walk you to your car,' he said, when Chrissy was near enough. 'For safety's sake.'

Chrissy made a show of peering around the carpark. 'Spot Todd hiding in the bushes, did you?'

'Nah, but you can't be too careful.'

'No, I suppose you can't.' She studied him, amusement tilting one corner of her mouth. 'Did you have a good night?'

'Yeah, it was great. Mum enjoyed it. Good job all round, especially from the waitressing staff.'

She laughed softly. 'Thanks.'

A laugh, that was progress. They shared a smile, then the restaurant's interior lights flicked off, darkening the carpark further.

Chrissy glanced at the building and then at her car, and shifted her handbag higher up on her shoulder. 'Look, Nick, it was sweet of you to hang around, but I've had a really long day. I just want home and sleep.'

Shit. A fob-off. To be fair, he could see she was tired, which was understandable given she'd been on her feet all night.

'Sure. We can talk while I walk you.' A conversation that'd be lucky to last seconds, but twenty metres to turn things around was better than nothing. 'So, you work in the restaurant as well as the winery?'

'Not normally. Our regular waitress called in sick, and with Yvette and Alistair away in Adelaide there was no one else to fill in. Shaun asked if I could help and I said yes.'

'Good of you.'

'I don't mind. Shaun's been great and Kai – he's the chef – has been a sweetheart from day one. I'd hate to see him left in the lurch and it's not like I don't have the experience. Waitressing helped put me through uni and marketing the restaurant is part of my position. Won't hurt me to get a feel for normal operations. Well,' she said, indicating her car, 'here we are.' Her mouth quirked. 'Again.'

'Yeah, here we are.'

'No Todd.'

He smiled. 'No. Just me.'

For a second she smiled back, then her keys jangled as she fidgeted with them. 'What are you doing here, Nick?'

He rubbed the back of his neck. This 'going for it' business wasn't as easy as it sounded. He sighed and dropped his arm. 'Probably making a peanut of myself.'

'You're not doing too badly. And I'm the expert at that, remember?'

'Sorry.'

'Don't. It was school. Like I said, life's moved on.'

'Moved on enough to come out with me Friday night? Wherever you like.'

'Nick ...' She took a breath. 'I can't. Sorry.'

Nick said a mental 'shit' and shoved his hands into his pockets. 'Boyfriend, I suppose.'

'Girlfriend, actually.'

He blinked. Seriously? She was gay? But ... what about her crush and all the things she did, the notes and calls and parades? Nick racked his peabrain for an appropriate response and could find nothing that wouldn't end up making him look insensitive.

He cleared his throat. 'Lucky girl.'

'Girls, to be precise.' At his boggle-eyed expression, Chrissy laughed. 'I'm meeting Paige and Alice at the Arms on Friday night. Maybe I'll see you there?'

Oh, right. Those kinds of girlfriends.

He rubbed his jaw as the idea he'd had earlier began to take firmer shape. 'Friday night at the Arms? Yeah, I reckon I can make that.'

———

'Operation Get Laid,' whispered Nick's brother in a terrible eastern European accent, 'zis ist go.'

Nick's stomach leaped at Danny's words, even as the 'Get Laid' bit annoyed him. This wasn't about getting laid. Not much, anyway.

'She with anyone?' he asked.

'Ya. Alice Lindner unt Paige de Bruin.'

Good. An audience would make this work all the better. 'Where?'

'Ze back bar near ze fire.'

'Settled in for a while?'

'How the hell should I know?' said Danny, dropping the accent. 'Barry's looking after that area. I only spotted her because I went to do a glass run. Shit, hang on.' There was a rustling noise that Nick guessed was from Danny pressing the phone against his chest as he dealt with the interruption. 'Look, we're flat out and I gotta go. You want to do your parade? Get your arse down here pronto.'

Nick was out the door before Danny had hung up.

As Danny said, the pub was bustling, the front and back bars milling with people simply enjoying a drink, waiting for Friday-night footy to begin, or for a table in the bistro to become free.

Nick stood in the shadows of the hall leading to the rear exit, watching Chrissy with her friends and wishing his stomach would stop reacting to the smell of chips that kept wafting from the pub's kitchen. He'd been late out at the farm and it'd been hours since afternoon tea, but he'd been too nervous to eat more than a couple of dry biscuits since arriving home.

Chrissy was perched on one of the vinyl-covered stools the publican kept scattered in front of the fire, along with a couple of low tables, to make the area more relaxed and lounge-like. Her body was angled towards the door leading to the front bar, and every now and then she'd glance at it before looking quickly away. Nick prayed it was him she was searching for and not some other bloke. That'd really ruin his plan.

Whatever she and her friends were talking about, it was making them animated, with waving hands and laughter and plenty of drinking. From the almost empty bottle of red wine on the coffee table, they'd been at it for a while, too. Wine had stained Chrissy's lips a kissable red and her face was deeply flushed. She bent forward to say something and leaned back with a grin and a wink that shot straight to Nick's stomach and made him forget all about food.

This stunt was going to make him look like a peanut, but what the hell, Chrissy was worth it. Besides, looking like a peanut was the whole point.

He checked the crowd one last time and sucked in a deep breath, exhaled slowly and began his strut.

At first no one noticed, then heads began to turn. People stopped chatting and frowned at him. A few snickers sounded.

Oh yeah, he looked like a peanut all right, parading past Chrissy and her friends, wiggling his arse like someone had dumped oats down his trunks.

Nick kept his head up. They could laugh all they liked. The only thing that mattered was her reaction, and he was big enough to take whatever shit flew his way.

He slid his eyes to the side. Chrissy's brow was furrowed, her nose screwed up. Paige and Alice were staring at him open-mouthed, as if he'd grown another head. Or, from the way their eyes were lowered to his jeans, popping one out of his bum.

A panicked thought hit Nick: what if she didn't get it?

'You got something in your duds, Burroughs?' yelled some wag from the bar.

'Yeah, mate,' said Nick, shooting him a grin and giving an extra wiggle for emphasis. 'A great arse.'

Guffaws sounded, along with more sledging. Nick checked back on Chrissy and his fear subsided at the laughter glittering her eyes. He said a silent thanks to his heckler and added more oomph to his step as he about-faced and paraded past again, even closer.

He slowed in front of her group, exaggerating the waggle even more. Paige released a whoop while Alice clapped and blew him a kiss, but Chrissy merely smiled and shook her head.

More whoops and heckles followed him out of the bar, but Nick didn't care. Chrissy had seen and she'd understood. His feet felt so light he may as well be moonwalking.

Grinning the entire time, he snuck out the back door, circled the pub and re-entered through the front entrance.

'Congratulations on making a prize dick of yourself,' said Danny, sliding a beer towards him.

Nick took a long gulp. He deserved this beer. Hell, he deserved twenty of them. 'A dick? Nah. I thought I made a pretty good job of it myself. Got Chrissy's attention.'

'What did she say?'

'Nothing, just laughed.' Along with the rest of the pub, but so what?

'You think it worked?'

Nick shrugged and took another gulp. It had made her laugh, that was enough for the moment, and this was only the first on the long list of stunts he had planned. By the end, if they all went the way he hoped, she'd be more than laughing at him.

He smiled to himself. Yeah. Lots more than laughing.

'Jesus,' said Danny.

'What?'

'You.'

'What about me?'

His brother just made a face and went off to serve.

Nick rubbed his jaw, wondering what that was all about, and glanced at the telly, where a bunch of talking heads were dissecting the weekend's football games. He watched for a moment then, sensing someone close, turned around.

'Nice walk,' said Chrissy.

For a second his brain was so scrambled by her gorgeousness he couldn't speak. 'Glad it caught your attention.'

'Mm,' she said, then deliberately tilted sideways to survey his butt. 'Are they your best jeans?'

'Why?' He flexed his glutes. 'Not up to scratch?'

She pressed a finger to her mouth and took another long look before meeting his gaze. 'I suppose they're okay.'

Nick opened his mouth to protest – his fit arse looked good in these jeans – then he realised she was teasing and shut it again.

'Not a bad effort though,' she said. 'For a first try.'

'Pleased you think so. Drink?'

'Oh no,' she said, shaking a finger. 'You're going to have to do better than that. Much better.'

Nick laughed. Chrissy James was not only gorgeous and fun, she was on exactly the same wavelength. He leaned close, the delicious apricot scent of her almost deleting his brain of the words he was about to say, but he regathered and locked his gaze on hers.

'For you I plan to.'

THE CELLAR-DOOR BUZZER jolted Chrissy from her spreadsheet. In the three weeks she'd been at Ryan's, she could count on one hand the number of times the buzzer had sounded on a weekday. Most cellar-door business took place on weekends, when people had more time for tastings or were combining wine buying with a leisurely lunch. Mondays, according to Shaun, were the quietest of all.

Glad for the respite from her computer screen, Chrissy set down her pen and glanced out her office window.

And sucked in a breath.

Nick Burroughs was sauntering across the polished concrete floor with his hands in his pockets and trailing an air of pure broad-shouldered manliness. His head swivelled as he slowly took in the space, dark hair shiny and flickering the occasional bronze sun streak under the skylight. Spotting the main counter, he headed to it, slid a set of tasting notes towards him and peered down.

He was doing nothing except standing casually, looking as though he'd stepped straight off the farm, yet the sight of him sent Chrissy's heart crashing around her chest, just as it had all those years ago at school.

She slid her chair closer to the window and stared, confident the slant of the office's vertical blinds would shield her from view.

His hair was wind-messed, his clothes rumpled, his boots scuffed. Instead of the jeans and striped shirt of Friday night, he wore khaki trousers and a thick blue fleece jumper, but the work clothes did nothing to detract from his innate sexiness. If anything, they added to his appeal. He didn't need to dress to impress. Nick was a man whose self-assurance came from inside rather than from the clothes he wore, a man confident in his skin.

He slid the tasting notes away and ran his gaze around the room, then, as though sensing Chrissy's scrutiny, he lifted his eyes to her office.

She propelled the chair backwards and breathed hard. He couldn't have spotted her, yet the half-smile on his face told her Nick knew she was there, and was waiting.

He moved casually into the illuminated space beneath the cellar's skylight, his gaze never leaving the office window, and lifted his hands slightly, as if to say, 'Well?'

God, he was attractive, even more so than at school. Maturity had honed his masculine edges, filled out his shoulders, chest and legs and chiselled his jaw with a precision edge. Eyelashes of a thickness and density no mascara could ever match fringed beautiful brown eyes so velvet soft that looking at them was like being cuddled. Chrissy had lost count of the fantasies she'd had about those eyes. Of her and Nick lying face to face, staring at one another, lost in love.

Wanting him had been agony, an agony made worse by his indifference. But as she'd told the girls, that was all in the past. Chrissy was a grown woman now, with a degree, a career and, more importantly, life experience. Pretty faces and old crushes didn't cut it anymore. Nick was just another customer.

Just. Another. Customer.

She stood, smoothed down her hair and pinstripe pencil skirt, and stepped purposefully towards the door.

'Hello,' she called as she descended. 'What brings you here?'

'Seems I've developed a sudden interest in wine,' Nick replied with a grin. 'Thought I might start a collection. I hear Ryan's is the best in the district, so here I am.'

'A collection,' said Chrissy, walking towards him, her high heels clacking on the concrete floor. Normally she wore jeans, leather boots and a Ryan's logoed shirt and jumper to work, but she was meeting with some local restaurant owners this afternoon and wanted a more professional presence. 'Really.'

'Really,' he said, his gazing raking her from head to toe, lingering on her red silk shirt and form-fitting skirt, before settling on her face.

'How about that.'

'Yeah.' His grin broadened. 'How about that.'

Chrissy regarded him for a long moment then walked briskly behind the counter. 'As it happens, you heard correctly. Ryan's is without doubt the best producer in the district. It's also the longest established, and thanks to the quality of its wine has proved that the Levenham district is a winegrowing force to be reckoned with. The terroir here is unique, resulting in wines of uncommon elegance, in particular with our white varieties, like our trophy-winning riesling.'

His grin lost some of its certainty. 'Right.'

'You understand terroir?'

'Um, no.'

'Do you know anything about wine?'

Nick scratched the underside of his jaw. 'Nope.'

She'd thought as much. So, today's visit was another stunt. Chrissy wondered which one he was copying. Friday night had been obvious, once she'd recovered from her initial shock – the parade was an imitation of what she used to do to attract his attention, albeit more exaggerated and with public jeering.

Though she'd tried her hardest not to be affected, that Nick had been willing to embarrass himself for her sake in a pub – the Arms, where his brother worked, no less – had impressed her.

Paige and Alice had been more than impressed. Chrissy had done her best to calm them down, but Alice in particular had been beside herself at the romanticism of Nick's gesture, especially coming on the heels of him waiting at Ryan's to walk her to her car and his earlier heroics with Todd.

Nevertheless, that didn't mean Chrissy was about to get carried away by it.

It wasn't that she didn't think he was cute or sexy or nice. Chrissy knew Nick was all those things, it was just that she simply didn't feel ready for this. The breakup with Owen had hurt more than she'd let on, and she'd only been home a month and she had a new job that she needed to concentrate on.

And what if she put on weight again? Or somehow became plain and uninteresting, the sort of girl a man like Nick would walk straight past without noticing. Not that Chrissy planned for that to happen; still, the concern was lodged in the back of her mind.

Nick liked the way she looked now, and that was fine. Flattering even. But that was all surface stuff. Shallow. He didn't know her, and though she knew a lot about him, who's to say what his heart was truly like.

'So, an oenological innocent,' she said, drumming her fingers. 'Well, what sort of wine do you like? Red? White? Sparkling?'

'All of them?'

Chrissy sighed and shook her head. 'We're going to have to start from scratch, then.'

'Looks like it.' Nick's grin was back to full wattage.

She eyed him for a long moment, then grabbed two glasses from below the counter and held them to the light to check their cleanliness. Satisfied, she placed one in front of him and kept the other for herself. 'We'll start with the sparkling.'

Chrissy talked as she fetched the bottle from the bar fridge below the counter, explaining Shaun Ryan's choice to use a blend of chardonnay and pinot noir rather than the usual straight pinot, and how the limestone-rich soil gave the wine a unique flavour and texture.

She poured a small sample for them both, lifted her glass and tapped the bowl. 'See how finely beaded the bubbles are? How they rise to the surface in delicate columns? They're called rosaries and are a good indication of quality. Now look at the colour. See that brightness?'

He nodded.

'It looks like a lively wine, doesn't it?'

'Lively?'

'Yes, as in fresh-looking, like it'll spring onto your palate and fill your mouth with flavour.'

Nick looked again, this time properly. 'Yeah, I suppose it does look lively.' He tilted his glass back and forth, catching it in the light. 'It's a bit glittery, sort of. Like in spring, when morning dew shivers on the fence lines, and the sun is rising and the breeze is just right. The droplets change to all these different colours as they fall.' He winced and coloured slightly. 'That's probably stupid.'

'No. That's good.'

In fact, it was a lovely description, and surprising. She hadn't expected Nick to come up with something so poetic. The idea that he'd notice such a little thing spread warmth through her, and for few heartbeats all Chrissy could think was what it would be like to see something like that with him. Standing in the dawn, hand in hand, as the world glittered magically around them.

Oh, this was so not good. Chrissy could feel her crush turning like a butterfly in its chrysalis, trying to break out. She had to stop it. Now.

Shoving her nose into her glass, she inhaled deeply and with a gesture, encouraged Nick to do the same. 'Okay, tell me what you smell?'

He took a cautious sniff. 'I don't know.'

'A bready, yeasty aroma perhaps?'

He sniffed again, this time inhaling deeper. He smiled. 'Yeah, I can smell it. Sort of like toast.'

'Now take a sip. Try to coat all of your mouth with the wine so it passes over all your tastebuds. Feel the creaminess of it.'

Chrissy tasted her own sample, and her eyes hooded slightly as she concentrated on the flavours. She hadn't been lying about the quality of Ryan's wines. The sparkling was superb, beautifully moussed and with plenty of character. With its modest price, it was exceptional value, too, a competitive advantage she planned to push in her meetings this afternoon.

She worked the tiny sip around her mouth some more and swallowed. Normally she'd use the spittoon, but the amount was barely enough to wet her mouth as it was, and she wasn't sure Nick was ready for that.

When she finished tasting she found Nick staring at her with his glass half-poised, his body tense. Chrissy touched her tongue to her lips to check for spilled drops but could feel nothing.

She frowned. 'Aren't you going to taste yours?'

He blinked and the tension eased. 'Yeah, sure.' He took a mouthful and nodded. 'It's good. Really good.'

'It is. It's quite unusual in that it has an almost maritime flavour, but that's the impact of the soil and the vineyard's proximity to the coast. We're only twenty or so kilometres from the sea as the crow flies here.'

Nick set down his glass. 'I'll take two bottles.'

'Only two?' she teased. 'Surely you need a whole case?'

He laughed. 'For you I'd buy ten dozen cases, but two'll do me for the moment.'

'If you're worried about your shoulder I could carry it out for you.'

'Nothing to do with my shoulder. I could lift a case of wine one-handed if needed.' He tilted his head towards his flexed bicep and winked, causing Chrissy's heart to perform a lazy somersault. Although covered by fleece, the bulge was pronounced. She had a feeling she'd be thinking about his muscles for the rest of the afternoon now, damn him.

Quickly turning away from that too-appealing bulge, she fetched his bottles and set them next to the till, then crouched to take the riesling out of the fridge, grateful for the cool air on her burning cheeks.

But when she unscrewed the cap and went to pour, Nick placed his hand over the top of his glass.

'That's fine. I'll just take the sparkling.'

'Oh.' There were still six wines to try, more if she snuck in some of the museum wines not normally available for tasting. She bit her lip and slid the tasting notes back and forth with the tip of her finger. 'But I thought you'd want to try them all.'

Then buy the lot, as she'd done with his raffle tickets all those years before.

'Nah, that's enough for one day.' He dragged a wallet from his back pocket and pulled out a credit card. 'I should get going.'

Chrissy tucked her hair behind one ear, wondering what she'd done wrong. Nick had seemed perfectly cheerful, but now it was like he couldn't wait to get out of the place. The disappointment was ridiculous.

She rang up the purchase, placing the bottles into a Ryan's bag as Nick used the credit machine, and pushed the wine towards him. 'I hope you enjoy them.'

'Don't worry, I will.' Then he winked, gathered up his wine and sauntered off, leaving Chrissy staring after him, baffled.

———

'You make the best coffee,' Chrissy told Kai as she sipped her latte.

'I do.' He pushed a plate towards her. 'And the best macaroons.'

Chrissy groaned. 'I shouldn't.'

'You should.'

'I'm going to end up so fat.'

'They are but air,' he said, waving a hand.

'And sugar. Don't forget that bit.'

Kai gave one of his affected Gallic shrugs. 'Sugar, air, these are the necessities of life.'

'So you keep telling me.' She sighed and bit into a macaroon. Her eyes rolled back in her head as flavour exploded in her mouth. Salted caramel macaroons. If he weren't already married, twenty years older and not remotely her type, Chrissy would be in love. 'God, that's good.'

'I know.'

She laughed and swatted a hand at the chef only to jolt as the buzzer to the cellar door sounded. 'Of all the timing.'

Kai checked the window. 'It's that Burroughs lad. The one who was here yesterday.'

Chrissy peered past him and groaned. Nick was leaning with one elbow on the counter and his body turned towards her office. He was dressed again in farm clothes and looked as ruggedly handsome as the previous day.

'God, what's he doing back here?'

'Is there a problem?'

'What?' Chrissy caught Kai's concern and patted his shoulder. 'No, it's fine.'

'Are you sure? If he's hassling you I'll take care of him.'

'He's not hassling me.' She glanced at Nick again. One corner of his mouth was turned up in a lazy smile. She wished he wouldn't do that. That smile had made her hormones crazy at school, which was fine for school. Ryan's was her workplace. Hormones needed to stay out of it.

Kai glanced over her shoulder at Nick then inspected her face. A smile broke out. 'Ah.'

Chrissy's eyes narrowed. 'What do you mean, ah?'

'Nothing, nothing.' He picked up her coffee and macaroons and began to walk out with them.

'Where are you going with those?' she asked, feeling

slightly outraged. She'd been looking forward to that coffee and more delicious nibbling.

'You're going to be busy for a while. The coffee will only go cold.' He grinned. 'Don't worry, I'll make you another.'

'But my macaroons.'

'Hostages.'

'What?'

'The price for all the gossip about your new admirer.'

Chrissy threw a pen at him, but Kai ducked easily out of range, his laughter carrying down the corridor as he sped her morning tea away. Taking another half-minute to compose herself, she headed for the stairs.

'You're back,' said Chrissy as she moved towards the counter.

'I am.' He tilted his head slightly, as if unsure what to make of her attitude. 'Thought I'd try the riesling.'

'You could have done that yesterday.'

He shrugged. 'I had to get back to work.'

Chrissy set out one glass, wondering why she was being so short. From the looks he was throwing her, Nick was asking himself the same thing.

'Not joining me today?'

'No.'

He pursed his lips and rocked slightly on his heels. 'Look, Chrissy, if me being here is going to cause a problem I'll go.' He smiled crookedly. 'I just wanted to ... you know.'

'No, I don't know.'

'I just thought this might be a good way to spend time with you, that's all.' Looking away, he shrugged again and Chrissy realised he was embarrassed. 'Get to know you properly. Maybe for you to get to know me a bit.' He paused. 'If you wanted.'

Oh, God, when he looked like that, all sheepish and sweet and unsure, she wanted. She wanted big time.

Chrissy's apology was cut short by Shaun Ryan appearing at the cellar-door entrance.

'Nick,' he said, striding towards Nick with his hand held out. Shamrock trotted at his heel like a shaggy miniature horse. 'How's things? Shoulder on the mend?'

They shook and immediately fell into a discussion about Nick's recovery and Mount Pitt's chances this season. As far as Chrissy knew Shaun didn't play, but football was a local religion and at this time of year Levenham was deep in its fever.

'So, what brings you here?' asked Shaun.

Nick shot Chrissy a glance. She widened her eyes, begging for him to not embarrass her in front of her new boss.

'Danny and Beth invited me around for a barbecue,' he said smoothly. 'Thought I'd grab some wine to take along.'

Shaun nodded at Chrissy. 'Chrissy here will see you straight. She knows her stuff. We're fortunate to have her on board. Anyway, I'd better get back to it. Good luck for Saturday.' And with a farewell wave, he strode off, Shamrock following.

Chrissy let out a breath, staying quiet until her boss was well out of earshot. 'Thanks.'

'I'm not here to embarrass you. That's the last thing I want.' Nick scuffed the front of his boot on the concrete floor, fists shoved deep into his pockets. 'Time for Plan B, I guess.'

'What was Plan A?'

'Turn up every day, taste a bit of wine, buy a couple of bottles until I'd gone through everything on the list.' He regarded her from under lush lashes. 'Talk a bit. I'm so used to doing my own thing on the farm I didn't think to factor in that this was your workplace. Sorry.'

'That's okay.' She fiddled awkwardly with a bottle opener. 'And Plan B?'

Nick checked around him, then leaned across the bar, gaze flicking from Chrissy's eyes to her mouth and back again, making her pulse race. 'I guess you'll have to wait and see.'

NICK FINISHED STACKING the new wine rack he'd bought that afternoon with the bottles he'd purchased from Ryan's, his mind on Chrissy and his next move.

He was still kicking himself over the winery stunt. Why hadn't it occurred to him that she might find his visits uncomfortable? Of course she wouldn't appreciate it. It was her frigging workplace, for crying out loud. Yet, when he'd first come up with the idea, Nick had thought it brilliant. He'd get to see her every day, find out more about her. And when it came to Chrissy he wanted to know everything.

Nick had felt so shitty about embarrassing her he'd bought a case of mixed whites and one of reds before he left. What the hell he was supposed to do with two cases of wine on top of the two bottles of sparkling he already had, he had no idea.

Invite Chrissy around so she could explain all about them in his own private tasting session?

He paused and smiled at the thought. He'd like learning from Chrissy, hearing her talk cleverly about things like terroir in that slightly husky voice of hers, watching her eyes hood and her lips glisten as she swirled wine around her mouth, the smooth skin of her neck moving as she swallowed. He'd like even more to kiss her wine-sweetened mouth afterwards.

The door banged, snapping his fantasy apart.

'Dude,' said Chops, walking in and throwing his keys on the table before heading straight for the fridge, as was his habit. A waft of cow shit and milk from his dad's dairy farm, where Chops worked, followed. He shoved a container of fresh milk in the door shelf and peered around inside, then suddenly turned to Nick with a stunned-mullet look on his face. 'Is that ...'

'Yeah, it's a wine rack.'

Chops shut the fridge door and scratched his scruffy brown hair. 'Dude?'

'Long story.'

Chops stared at the rack, then the boxes, then at Nick. 'Ryan's.'

Conversation had never been his housemate's forte.

'Yeah, Ryan's. Where Chrissy works.'

'And she ...' He waved at the rack with a slightly horrified expression, as if to ask, 'A *girl* made you do this?' Which was a bit rich when Stacey had Chops twisted so tight around her finger she had him doing far dumber things than buying wine and furniture to store it on, but that was love for you.

'Nah, that was me. Fucked up and embarrassed her at work, so I bought a couple of cases to help make up for it.'

'Right,' said Chops, although he clearly didn't think it was right at all. 'Your poison, dude.' Then he reopened the fridge, extracted a beer and wandered off.

Nick spent the rest of the evening brainstorming ways to get Chrissy's attention using the clues she'd given him.

He'd done the arse strut, and from her amused reaction that was a definite tick in the positives box. The raffle-ticket equivalent had ended in disaster. He did have a rack full of costly wine, which could be counted as some sort of match, but Nick doubted Chrissy would see it that way.

Which left cards in lockers, notes in sports bags and phone calls.

Phone calls were out because at this point they'd be creepy rather than fun, and Nick didn't know Chrissy's number anyway.

Cards in her letterbox? Jesus, no. That'd be even worse than phone calls.

He was stuck with notes in her sports bag, but did she even play sport? She looked like she did. You didn't get a figure like hers without doing at least some exercise. Chrissy had mentioned playing netball at school when they talked in the carpark after the Todd incident, but that didn't mean she played now.

Netball. He imagined her in one of those tight uniforms, little skirt skimming the very tops of her thighs, legs and chest pink from exertion, then had to give himself a mental smack before he got too lost in the fantasy.

A pity Beth didn't play netball or Nick could ask her to find out if Chrissy did, but Beth was as bad as his brother, working all the time. Although at least Danny still had time for footy. Mind you, Danny didn't have much choice in that. The entire club would string him up if he tried to quit.

Nick stared broodily at the television as he mulled it over. Chops was on the phone to Stacey, using more words with her in one conversation than he'd use in a week with Nick. They could spend hours talking, mostly about shit if the snippets Nick caught were anything to go by. Nick used to talk to Leah like that when they first started going together, but that ended when their relationship began to peter out.

He let out a long sigh. Nothing for it, he was going to need help.

'Hey,' he said, interrupting Chops mid-flow, 'do me a favour and ask Stace if she has Alice Lindner's or Paige de Bruin's number.'

Chops threw him an annoyed look but did as Nick asked. He listened for a moment, then smiled slyly. 'Stace says to ask Leah.'

Nick should have guessed she'd say that. 'Yeah, thanks. Tell her I'll remember that next time she wants me out of the house so you two can bang yourselves stupid.'

Bugger. He'd have to ring Leah. Then Leah would tell all her mates, and everyone in town who hadn't already worked it out from his pub arse parade would know he had the hots for Chrissy. Worse, Connor would probably learn Nick had phoned Leah and the peanut would get the wrong idea again and it'd be on, and unlike Todd, Connor was no flabby fat-boy pushover.

He really needed his shoulder to get better. Or get the girl.

Nick could beat the world if he had the girl.

———

Nick leaned against the door of his ute and tapped the edge of the envelope against his fist, his breath steaming in the cold night air as he waited for Alice.

He stopped his tapping and ran his finger over the envelope's seal, doubting again what he'd written, wondering whether it was enough or too stupid. Whether he should have stuck to his original plan and bought a standard greeting card from the newsagent instead of letting Josh Sinclair's wife, Em, con him into buying a card-making kit from her shop PaperPassion.

His original plan had seemed straightforward until then. Choose a romantic card, not too silly or soppy, but with enough meaning to show he was serious about his feelings, add a few words of his own and job done.

Except he'd made the mistake of thinking Em might have something a bit more special and walked out with a kit containing a set of six blank cards, coloured pens, stickers, glitter and matching paper. Though it made him feel like a dill, Nick had become so addicted to creating the perfect card for Chrissy he'd ended up working well into the small hours on it.

What was meant to be a simple message had turned into a red, white and pink confection of layered flower cut-outs, sparkly butterflies and rainbows, and a glued-on satin bow, with the words 'This Is Pretty' on the front and 'But You're Prettier' on the inside, followed by 'Your not very secret admirer' and his phone number. All written in glittery dark-pink ink.

It was cringeworthy and corny and so embarrassing it made Nick's skin heat whenever he thought of it, but that was the whole point. He was meant to embarrass himself, suffer the same agonies she had at school. Nick just hadn't realised it'd be this bad.

He breathed out as a car pulled into the park beside his. Alice waved through the window, then turned off the engine and stepped out. She was a nice girl with a giant personality that belied her tiny size. When Nick had phoned asking for help, she couldn't say yes quickly enough.

'I'm so sorry I'm late,' she said, sounding flustered. 'This Show Queen challenge is taking up more time than I ever imagined.' She smiled, a cute dimple forming on her right cheek. 'I'm not usually this competitive, but I want to win really badly.'

'This is the Art Week thing?' Each year in the spring, Levenham hosted an arts festival and this year a wine fair had been added to the final weekend. If the local *Levenham Leader* newspaper was to be believed, it was going to be huge. In celebration of the inaugural fair, the committee had designed a Miss Levenham–style competition to raise money for charity. To stop it being branded sexist, ageist or any other 'ist', it was open to all locals, regardless of age or sex, with the winner being whoever raised the most money. The prize was nothing more than the kudos of being crowned Levenham Wine Show queen or king.

A few people had grumbled about the old-fashioned nature of it, but the majority of the town's population thought the idea a bit of fun and a great way to raise money for local causes. With nearly a dozen entrants, the competition was surprisingly fierce.

She nodded. 'It's not that I have a crown fetish or anything. I want to do it for Mum.' For a brief moment her expression turned wistful, and Nick gave himself a mental reminder to donate a couple of hundred dollars to her fund, and tell the rest of his family to do the same. It was the least he could do as thanks for her help, and that fleeing look of sorrow made him want Alice to win even more. Then she smiled and clapped her hands together. 'You and Chrissy. I love what you're doing. It's so sweet.'

'Yeah, well, I just hope Chrissy thinks so.'

'She will.' Alice indicated the card. 'Is that it?'

'Yeah.' Nick tapped it against his fist, reluctant to hand it over, knowing he needed to.

'She'll love it, Nick. I promise.'

He sighed and passed it. 'I hope so.'

Alice turned the envelope over and Nick's face heated as she traced the glittery pink of Chrissy's name with her finger. 'In her sports bag you say, not her handbag?'

'Yeah. It's where she—' He stopped. Maybe Chrissy wouldn't want him spilling all her secrets, even to Alice.

'Where she used to put her notes to you.' She patted his arm. 'It's okay. I know all about the notes and cards, and other things. She had such a terrible crush on you.'

Nick wished she still had it.

'Pity I was too much of a jerk to notice.'

Alice cocked her head. 'Did you really not notice her?'

'Yeah, as stupid as it sounds I didn't. I mean, I did sort of. It wasn't like she was invisible or anything, but I didn't notice her, you know, like that.'

'Because she was a bit overweight?'

'Yeah, probably.' He made a wry face. 'Like I said, I was a jerk.'

'I think she understands. We were all a bit silly at school and you're making up for it now. Nick,' she said, her tone suddenly serious, 'can I ask you something?'

'Sure.'

'This is real, isn't it? Not some sort of game? Only Chrissy's had a bit of a hard time recently and we'd hate to see her hurt again.'

'What do you mean a hard time?'

Alice hesitated. 'Her last boyfriend ... He wasn't good to her.'

Nick's eyes narrowed. 'Explain "not good".'

'He had a one-night stand with a girl from work after a drinks party, and when Chrissy found out he couldn't figure out what she was so upset about when he was drunk and it didn't mean anything.'

'What the fuck?' Nick's chest swelled hot with anger. What sort of peanut cheated on a girl like Chrissy, and then thought it was okay because he was hammered? Someone with no balls, that's who. No wonder Chrissy was wary. 'Well, that's not me. Ever.'

And he frigging meant it, too. He was a Burroughs, and if there was one thing a Burroughs knew, it was how to be a man.

Glittery cards with flowers and butterflies notwithstanding.

Alice smiled. 'I thought you'd say that. Leah told Paige you were the loveliest boyfriend she'd ever had. Besides Connor, that is.'

Nick had to stop himself from snorting. He bet he ran rings around Connor in the boyfriend stakes. Leah wasn't still friends with Nick because he'd been a dickhead.

'I think it's so romantic what you're doing for Chrissy,' said Alice on a deep sigh. 'I wish someone would do something like this for me. Never mind.' She waggled the envelope. 'I'll make sure she gets this. And if there's anything else I can do to help, let me know, okay?'

'Thanks, Alice.' Nick bent to kiss her cheek. 'You're a doll.' He opened the car door for her and shut it when she settled inside and started the engine.

The envelope lay on the passenger seat, Chrissy's pink name even more glittery in the dim light of the car's dashboard. He watched Alice's car all the way out of the carpark before hopping into his own.

Pink glitter. Jesus. What the hell was he thinking?

EIGHT

CHRISSY RUMMAGED in her bag for a towel to wipe the sweat from her forehead and frowned when the back of her hand scratched against the corner of something hard and unfamiliar. She pulled the bag wider and pushed her Levenham Rebels hoodie out of the way to expose what it was.

A cream-coloured envelope was wedged between a spare pair of socks and a roll-on deodorant. The paper had the thick, rippled look of high-quality stock, and bulged slightly from whatever was inside.

She looked up and around. Wallace Park was crowded with players, officials and spectators rugged up against the cold. Her teammates were drinking from water bottles and congratulating themselves on their win. Paige was with the coach, sweaty and red-faced from the game. She mimed a pass then a shot at goal before grinning madly. Alice was near her own kit bag, gulping down water, her attention intent on the game on the next court.

Too intent.

Chrissy's eyes narrowed on her friend and back at the

envelope. Using the tip of one finger, she tilted it until she could read the front. Her name was spelled out in sparkly pink letters.

Glitter pen? Was he serious?

Yet she couldn't help smiling. She'd been wondering what trick Nick would try next and had expected some sort of message, but not one using pink glitter pen. She pushed the envelope to the bottom of the bag and extracted the towel and wiped her face, then snatched out her hoodie and water bottle and went to interrogate Alice.

'Bumped into Nick, did you?'

'What makes you ask that?' Alice's blink was pure innocence, but Chrissy wasn't fooled.

'Don't you try to pull that butter-wouldn't-melt look with me. There's an envelope in my bag. How do you suppose it got there?'

'I don't know. Fairies?'

Chrissy tipped her bottle at Alice. 'The only fairy around here is you.'

Alice finally dropped her act and let her excitement shine through. 'Did you open it? What did it say? It's so romantic, Nick copying all the things you did. You're so lucky. He's a complete darling.'

'Who is?' asked Paige, wandering over and sliding her arms into her jacket.

'Nick, who else?' said Alice, smiling dreamily. 'He's left a card in Chrissy's bag.'

'Correction,' said Chrissy, copying Paige with her own Rebels hoodie. The day was overcast, with a nasty southerly, and though she was still sweating she'd soon chill. With the new projects she was balancing at work, the last thing Chrissy needed was a cold. 'The leaving was all you.'

'Someone has to play cupid,' said Alice, pouting.

'Well,' said Paige, looking at Chrissy, 'what did it say?'

Chrissy shrugged and deliberately took her time zipping up her jacket before taking a long drink. 'Haven't opened it.'

Paige rolled her eyes at Alice. 'She's so frustrating.'

'She is.' Alice leaned close to Paige, her grin so gleeful it was borderline evil, which was quite an achievement for someone of Alice's sweet looks. 'He wrote her name on it using pink glitter pen.'

'You're kidding me?'

'Nope.' Alice was fairly squirming with the delight of it. 'And that was just the front. Imagine what's on the inside.'

'He's a man, Alice,' said Chrissy. 'It's hardly going to be an essay.'

And she was right, as Chrissy discovered when she finally made it to the privacy of her car and, unable to wait any longer, slid a fingernail under the envelope's seal and pulled the contents into her lap.

Like the envelope, the card was thick cream stock. Across the front was a kind of flower posy made of not-very-neat cut-outs, stuck on in multiple layers so they stood proud from the surface. Floating around it Nick had clumsily drawn birds using more glitter pen, and stuck stickers of rainbows and butterflies with multicoloured wings. Glued to the posy's base was a piece of fine satin tape knotted into a sloppy bow.

Chrissy read the 'This Is Pretty' text and, with her heart beating like she was still in the middle of a netball game, opened the card to read the rest of his message.

'But You're Prettier'.

Was he for real? Groan-worthy didn't come close to describing it.

She let out a noise that was a half-laugh half-scoff. It

was completely and utterly ridiculous. So ridiculous it was almost childlike. Yet for all that it was also funny and heart-tugging, and left her feeling warm and more than a little bit soppy-sentimental.

Nick Burroughs had actually made her a card. Not bought one. Made it. And from the number of individually glued cut-outs and other decorations, it must have taken him ages.

She should be over the moon, fluttering like the butterflies in his picture, and yet ...

Chrissy sat back, staring out of the windscreen at nothing, and chewed on her lip, wondering why she suddenly felt so flat. What did she expect, an 'I love you'? That wasn't going to happen and nor did she want it to. Nick knew nothing about her. Telling her he loved her would be weird.

She sighed and traced the tip of her finger around 'But You're Prettier'. Chrissy had been pretty in school, too, beneath the braces and bad hair and round face. He just hadn't noticed. Not only not noticed her looks, but her entire self. This in a period when she'd been mad for him in that agonising, intense way that defined teenage crushes, and had placed herself in his orbit at every opportunity. It had hurt, and despite her protests otherwise, she was finding it still did.

The irony was that her hurt now was different. He was seeing her all right, bright and clear. But that was only the surface her, and experience had taught her that a relationship needed more to grow and survive than mutual attraction. It needed friendship and trust and liking.

There was no question that Nick was a darling, as Alice had said, but he still had a long way to go before Chrissy would feel safe enough to succumb to that well-honed Burroughs boy charm.

———

'Come on,' said Alice, linking her arm with Chrissy's and Paige's as they made their way across the sports-centre carpark the following Friday night, after a brief Rebels team meeting. 'Let's go to the pub.'

'I shouldn't,' said Chrissy, although the thought of possibly bumping into Nick made her heart stutter. 'I've had a really long week and we have a game tomorrow.'

'A couple of drinks won't hurt,' said Paige. 'Didn't do any harm last week.'

'Or the week before,' said Alice, squeezing her arm. 'And I'll buy.'

Chrissy gave Alice a suspicious look. 'This had better not be one of your tricks.' She wouldn't put it past them, especially Alice.

'Nope, purely spur of the moment.'

'It'd better be.'

'Why are you being so funny about Nick anyway,' said Paige. 'I thought you thought the card was cute.'

'It was.'

'And?' asked Alice, poking her.

'And nothing. It was one card.' She gave a haughty sniff. 'I sent him at least four.'

More, actually, now that she thought of it, and that was just the cards. There were the little notes to count as well. God, she'd been pathetic.

'Must do better, huh?' said Paige, laughing at her.

'Exactly.'

'Well, I think it was gorgeous of him to send one, and a handmade one at that. There aren't too many men in this world who'd do that.'

Which only made Chrissy feel bad, because Alice was

right. There weren't many men in the world like Nick and she really should have personally thanked him. Given the effort he'd gone to, he probably anticipated – and deserved – a text message at least. Instead, knowing Alice would likely pass it on, Chrissy had commented that she thought the card was cute and left it at that.

Spotting Danny behind the bar at the Arms, Alice immediately dived into a gap and popped up grinning in front of him. Chrissy towed Paige to the back bar and managed to nab some seats in the corner to the side of the fire. Not as cosy as right in front, but it offered a good view of the pub. The icy wind that had plagued the district the previous Saturday was back, and after their walk across the carpark, any place close to the fire was welcome.

'Can't see him,' said Paige, who'd been sweeping her gaze around the pub.

'Who?'

'Who do you think? Nick, of course, and like you haven't been looking too.'

Chrissy had, but she wasn't about to admit it.

Alice arrived with drinks. The girls chinked wine-glasses, toasting their netball team and wishing another good win for tomorrow, before settling in to a long discussion about Alice's fundraising efforts and what else they could do to help. It seemed like no time before their glasses were empty.

Chrissy rose. 'I'll get this round.'

'I said I was buying!'

'Leave her,' said Paige. 'She just wants to check if Nick is here.'

'Do not.'

'Do so!'

Chrissy threw her friend a fake sneer and gathered up the glasses.

'We'll keep an eye out this side then, shall we?' shouted Paige to her back, when Chrissy headed off. If it weren't for the wineglasses she was carrying, Chrissy would have flipped her the finger.

Friday-night football had kicked off, easing the crowd at the bar as patrons wandered off to stare at the big screen and yell commentary. Chrissy slipped into a gap nearest to where Danny was serving and waited. Normally she wouldn't care who served her, but Chrissy was feeling bad about Nick and maybe Danny might know how his brother was feeling about the whole thing. Assuming Nick had discussed it with him.

Spotting her, Danny shot Chrissy a 'don't move' gesture and went back to pulling beers. Clearly he had something to say. Chrissy wondered what it could be, and the anxiety of it made her look down and fiddle with the zipper of her handbag.

'Bugger me, it's Chrissy James. Long time, no see.'

Chrissy looked up, then up some more. 'Eddie.' She gave Alice's giant-sized ex-boyfriend a brief hug. She'd always liked him, even beyond his and Alice's breakup, the cause of which was cloaked in mystery. Other than saying he'd let her down badly, Alice had never really explained it. 'You've grown even taller since I last saw you.'

He hugged her back. 'Grown bigger muscles, too. Want to see them?'

She laughed. Eddie's flirty nature hadn't changed, then. 'Thanks, but I'll give it a miss.'

'I hear you're working at Ryan's now.'

'Uh-huh. Marketing and customer service manager, and loving every minute so far.'

'Sounds impressive. Glad to be home, then?'

'Yeah.' She smiled. 'I didn't realise how much I missed the place until now. And it's great to be close to my family again.'

'Jesus, Chrissy, don't talk to him,' interrupted Danny. 'He's a sleaze.'

'Am not,' said Eddie, puffing out his chest.

'Are so,' chorused two voices behind them.

When Chrissy jerked round, she discovered that one belonged to an unusually fiery-eyed Alice.

The other was Nick's.

NICK HAD BEEN SLOUCHED in front of the telly watching football when his phone signalled a text message. For a heart-stopping moment before he focused properly, he thought it might be Chrissy, then his brother's name flashed on the screen and his excitement died. Nick had checked his phone a bazillion times already this week and there'd been nothing from her. Why should tonight be any different?

He considered ignoring it and then couldn't help himself.

Chrissy back bar, the message said.

It was a short drive to the Arms and for every second of it Nick had half panicked that he'd walk in and discover she'd already left with some other bloke. He doubted it, but it was still a mad thought and his ego had taken a hell of a bruising that week. Not a phone call, not even a text message. Only a short chat with Alice on Sunday night in which she'd assured him Chrissy had read his card and said it was cute but was refusing to talk any more about it. Alice thought she was being unusually close-mouthed.

Which didn't sound good to Nick.

It was the bloody pink glitter pen. He'd known it was too much, yet he'd still gone ahead with it. Idiot.

Nick used the rear carpark entrance and immediately spotted Paige and Alice near the fire, but no Chrissy. As he paused to check the rest of the room, Alice rose and headed through the door to the front. Figuring maybe she was heading to help Chrissy carry drinks, he followed only to nearly crash into the back of her when Alice came to a sudden halt.

'Shit, sorry,' he said, but Alice wasn't listening. Her gaze was fixed at the end of the bar, where that thumping great peanut Eddie Argyle stood grinning down at a dark-haired girl.

A dark-haired girl who happened to be Chrissy.

'Fuck,' said Nick at the same time Alice muttered 'crap'.

As though pulled by the same force, they strode to the bar together, arriving just in time for Danny to call Eddie a sleaze and for Eddie to puff up like the cocky rooster he was and try to deny it.

'Are so,' said Nick in a way that made the words almost sound like 'arsehole'. He liked Eddie, but seeing him near Chrissy made his head steam.

Eddie grinned, only for it to collapse completely when he spied Alice. 'Alice,' he said with a terse nod.

'Eddie,' replied Alice, equally coolly.

Chrissy's smile at Nick was short and worried, her focus immediately darting back between Alice and Eddie.

For a pause no one said anything, then Danny cleared his throat. 'Are you guys going to stand there like a bunch of bunnies or is anyone going to order?'

'Sorry,' said Chrissy, turning to the bar. 'Can I have—'

But before she could finish, Nick grabbed her hand. 'Can I have a quick word first?'

Alice pushed Chrissy towards him. 'You go with Nick. I'll get the drinks.'

Chrissy glanced at Eddie and back at Alice. 'Are you sure?'

'Yes. I said tonight was my shout.' Alice gave her another shove. 'Now go.'

'Only if you're sure.'

'Yes! Go!'

Nick could have kissed Alice, but right now he had other things to think about.

'Come on,' he said, and keeping hold of Chrissy's hand, threaded her between patrons and out into the Arms's main front entrance, where a grand timber staircase led to the function room above. He steered her to a dark nook between the stairs and what was now the poker-machine room, where a payphone he'd never seen anyone use languished.

Nick leaned his shoulder against the wall and faced her. It was as private a spot as he could get without carting her upstairs or outside, and it was too cold for that.

He studied Chrissy's face, worried what she might be thinking, whether he'd been too presumptuous in grabbing her hand and expecting her to follow blindly. Nick hadn't thought, he'd just acted, wanting her as far away from Eddie as possible. At least she'd yet to pull her hand from his. That had to be worth something.

'How are you?' he asked.

'Good. You?'

'Had better weeks.' He rubbed his thumb over the back of hers. 'Spent most of it checking my phone for messages, hoping you'd call.'

She shifted to press her back against the wall and closed her eyes briefly. 'I'm sorry. I should have. It was rude of me.'

'It was the glitter pen, wasn't it?'

She smiled and shook her head.

'Butterflies?'

That earned a soft chuckle.

'Yeah,' he said, nodding to himself. There was amusement in her expression now. 'The bow. I knew it was overkill.'

'It wasn't any of those things.'

The way she was leaning, with her head against the wall, exposed the pale skin of her throat. Nick wished they were at the stage where he could nuzzle it, but, amusement or not, trying that on right now would probably earn him a knee in the crown jewels.

'Then why didn't you call?'

She shifted around to lean her shoulder against the wall in a mirror pose to his, so close he caught a breath of her intoxicating apricot Chrissy smell. The urge to press his lips to her skin, to any part of her, tugged harder.

'Do you remember what I used to write in the cards I sent you?'

Nick swallowed. This was very dangerous ground. 'Not exactly.' He remembered a lot of flowery girly stuff and love hearts, and about how awesome she thought he was. 'It was a fair while ago, and I was a jerk. But I'm not a jerk now.'

She smiled a little and raised a single eyebrow. 'You sure about that?'

'Okay, so visiting you at work was a jerkish thing to do.' He shrugged. 'What can I say? You make me lose my brains and unlike you, I never had that many to start with.'

Whatever it was he'd said, it hit something. Biting her lip, she turned her face from his, avoiding his gaze.

'What? What's wrong?'

'It's nothing.'

'Come on, Chrissy, it's not nothing.'

A worrying number of seconds passed before she finally spoke, and when she did there was a definite smile in her voice. 'You know you're making it very hard for me not to fall for you again.'

Fall for him again? The thought alone made his heart do cartwheels.

'That's the aim.' He meant to make her laugh, but she shook her head and looked away. Nick didn't get what was wrong. Hadn't she just admitted she was struggling to resist him?

He waited for her to say something to help him out, but she seemed to be thinking hard. 'Chrissy?'

She let out a breath and rubbed her eyes, the action tired. A group of people passed the stairs, chattering loudly as they headed to the exit and out into the night, leaving a blast of frigid air from the opened door in their wake.

Chrissy let go of his hand and stepped from the wall. 'I should really be getting back.'

'Just a bit longer?'

'I can't. Paige will be wondering where I am, and I'm worried about Alice after that weirdness with Eddie at the bar.'

Nick wanted to argue further, but he had the sense that he'd pushed his luck already. 'Okay, I'll walk with you.'

'No, it's fine. I need to duck into the ladies' first.'

'Oh, right.' Bit bloody hard to follow into there, and he had the feeling it was just an excuse to get rid of him. Which stung. He'd thought they were doing okay there for a moment. He shoved his fists into his pockets and tried not to look sulky, but he bloody well felt sulky. She liked him, had as good as admitted it, so what was with the hurrying off? 'Good luck for tomorrow. Hope you win.'

She smiled over her shoulder. 'Thanks. I hope Mount Pitt does too.' She took two more steps and stopped. From the rise of her shoulders he could see she was breathing deeply, like a person fortifying themselves.

Nick waited, his heart doing crazy flip-flops.

Suddenly she whirled, and next thing he knew Chrissy was standing on tip-toe, gripping his shirt, her mouth so close to his it'd take a fraction of movement to kiss her.

'I sent you five cards,' she said, her gaze darting from his eyes to his mouth and back again. 'Five, and that's not including the notes.'

'And?'

'You have a lot of catching up to do.' She fisted her fingers tighter into his shirt and dragged him closer, head tilting as though angling for a kiss. Her breath touched his lips and shot an electric jolt straight to his groin. 'A lot.'

Then as quickly as she'd grabbed him, she was gone.

'Jesus,' Nick muttered, running his hand through his hair. '*Jesus.*'

That was unexpected. Unexpected but frigging fantastic. He threw his head back and laughed, then stopped when Connor Viccary pushed through the door, a mean look on his face, and that peanut Todd Leppington on his heels.

Connor was in his face in seconds. 'What's with calling Leah?'

'I needed to ask her for a number, that's all. I'm not interested in Leah.' Nick ducked his head to the side to smirk at Todd. 'Got another girl on my mind.'

Todd's expression turned mutinous.

Connor jabbed a finger at Nick's chest. 'You stay away from her.'

'Yeah. Whatever.' It would take more than a finger jab and mild threat to upset Nick right now. He batted aside Connor's hand and stepped past him. Time for home and some card making. Unable to resist, he winked at Todd as he sauntered by. 'Thanks, mate.'

'What the fuck for?'

'Chrissy, who else? Because of you, I've got the girl. Enjoy your night. I sure will.'

ALICE DIDN'T bother to be sneaky this time. She rolled up to netball training on Tuesday night and danced towards Chrissy with Nick's envelope held in front of her chest.

'Look what I-I-I have,' she sang, then ducked out of the way when Chrissy tried to swipe it. Alice then sidled up to Paige and pointed to the envelope's front. 'Look. Blue glitter pen. What do you think *that* could mean?'

'That could mean you getting your bottom spanked, young lady,' said Chrissy, unimpressed.

She'd been waiting for this since Friday night, and though she appreciated it would have taken some planning on Nick's part, Chrissy had still expected something from him on Saturday, when she'd turned up for netball. That there was nothing had left Chrissy's face burning even more than when she'd pulled that move at the Arms.

It had been sexy though, grabbing Nick's shirt like that, edging up on her toes to bring her mouth whisper close to his. He had smelled good. Even better had been the feel of his body against hers, and only sheer willpower had controlled her hammering urge to kiss him stupid. Her dreams that night had been rampant with him, wanton, leaving her restless and needy and wishing she had kissed him, even if only for a heartbeat. Then at least she'd know if what Leah had said about him being a fantastic kisser was true, rather than being driven crazy imagining it.

Neither Alice nor Paige cared about her frustration. They were too busy inspecting the envelope.

'The other one felt fatter,' said Alice, pressing it between her thumb and forefinger. She passed it over. 'You have a go.'

'Hmm,' said Paige, looking thoughtful as she assessed, then she lifted it to her nose and gave a good sniff. 'Nope, no aftershave.'

Chrissy stood with her arms folded and her weight on one hip. 'Have you two quite finished?'

Paige raised her eyebrows at Alice. 'Have we?'

'Not sure,' said Alice, taking back the envelope and holding it up to the sports ground's big arc lights to check if she could see anything inside. Her nose scrunched up as she peered, then she shook her head. 'I really can't see anything. Do you think we should give it to the lady in question to open?'

'Probably. She's looking a bit murderous.'

With a skip and a giggle Alice finally went to hand over the envelope, only to snap it away when Chrissy tried to take it. 'We want more than an "it's cute" this time.'

'Full report,' agreed Paige.

'You'll get what you're given,' said Chrissy, and in a sneaky-swift move, tackled Alice and wrestled the envelope from her grip. Then she bolted for her car, ignoring the calls of 'cheat' and 'sook' behind her, and locked it safely inside.

'You are being absolutely no fun,' said Alice when Chrissy returned.

'Says she who refuses to discuss Friday night's weirdness with Eddie.'

'That was not weirdness.'

'Could have fooled me.' Chrissy gave her a friendly nudge. 'It's okay though, isn't it?'

'Of course.'

'You sure?'

'Very. Who cares about him anyway? I have far bigger fish to fry. Now,' she said, looping her arm through Chrissy's, 'are you still set for Sunday?'

Chrissy let it slide. Alice knew very well she was set – it was Chrissy who had arranged the meeting with Kai to talk about catering for Alice's high tea fundraiser.

She managed to get through training without thinking too much about Nick's card, but every dropped catch or missed pass had her friends teasing anyway. To get them back, Chrissy left straight after, waving the envelope at them through the windscreen as she passed, and adding a horn honk for extra annoyance.

Though she fizzed with excitement, Chrissy left opening the card until she was showered and content with a belly full of leftover lasagne from the previous night's dinner with her sister and brother-in-law at her mum and dad's, and a glass of Ryan's cabernet sauvignon nearby.

She used her knife to slit the edge and pulled out the card.

And nearly choked on her laughter.

Nick had drawn a toothily grinning, rainbow-farting unicorn on the front of the card and decorated it with sparkles.

Still laughing, she opened the card to read what he'd written.

'Seeing you in the carpark at the Arms that first night left me more poleaxed than a rainbow-farting unicorn.'

Feeling silly, Chrissy hugged it to her chest then, before she could change her mind, snatched up Nick's original card with his phone number on it, and shot him a text message.

Not bad for a second effort.

Nick's reply took only seconds. *Wait till you see my third, baby.*

She laughed and tossed her phone aside. As tempting as it was to keep chatting, that was enough for one night.

Besides, she couldn't let him have things too easy.

———

Chrissy groaned at the plate Kai slid in front of her and covered her face with her hands. 'I said no more.'

'But it is only *petit*.'

'That,' she said, dropping her hands and pointing at the quadruple-layered chocolate-sponge concoction, complete with flakes of gold leaf on top, 'is not *petit*. There's enough sugar and fat in that to give a hippo cellulite.'

Kai sighed. 'You exaggerate.'

'I do not.'

'Do.'

'Look,' said Chrissy, pushing the plate back towards him, 'it's beautiful, it really is, and I bet it tastes incredible, like every other thing you make, but enough's enough. I can't eat it.' She leaned back and hooked a thumb into the waistband of her jeans and pulled. 'Look at this. When I started five weeks ago these were loose, now I can barely get my thumb in there. I have a muffin top, Kai. A bloody *muffin top*. The last time I had one of those was at school!'

Kai crossed his arms, his mouth set mutinously. 'You are not fat.'

'I know that, but surely even you can see I'm putting on weight?'

'No. I see a beautiful, healthy young woman who deserves a bit of joy and that,' he pointed to the plate, 'is joy.'

Chrissy groaned and slumped her head on the desk.

Kai patted her hair. 'I'll bring your coffee.'

Chrissy waved him off without looking up, and made a mental note to actually leave work on time tonight so she could jog a dozen extra laps of Wallace Park before netball training started.

She eased up. She hated jogging, it bored the pants off her, but netball training meant the possibility of another card from Nick, and if there was one thing Nick was proving to be, it was far from boring. Kai might think his sweet concoction was joy, but it had nothing on how Chrissy felt whenever she thought of Nick's card. Whenever she thought of Nick, for that matter.

Despite her hopes, Alice turned up at the courts empty-handed.

'Expecting something?' said Alice, all innocence.

Chrissy gave her a look. She was hot and sweating copiously in spite of the crisp night, and her feet ached from jogging on hard asphalt. Tonight was not a night for teasing.

Alice and Paige exchanged a glance and broke into giggles.

'Look at you,' said Paige, pointing. 'You'd swear your dog just died.'

Chrissy wiped her face on a towel and threw the damp cloth at Paige. 'Shut up.'

'Oh, come on, admit it. You've been hanging out all day for this, hoping Alice would have a present for you.'

Chrissy narrowed in on Alice. 'And do you?'

Alice twinkled her fingers as though playing an air piano and began to whistle.

'Not funny.'

'Yes, it is,' said Paige.

'It is,' agreed Alice.

Chrissy breathed through her nose, trying for calm. 'So where is it, then?'

'What?'

'Don't you give me that round-eyed look, madam,' said Chrissy, stalking towards Alice and snapping her fingers. 'Give.'

Alice frowned at Paige. 'Do you think we should?'

Paige tapped her chin a few times. 'No.'

'Yes, she's hardly shared, has she? I mean what's that now? Two cards? And we still don't know what he wrote.'

'Not very nice when we're her best friends and everything.'

'Indeed.'

Chrissy groaned. 'You two.'

'I know,' said Alice, slinging an arm around her. 'You love us to bits.'

Paige joined in from the other side. 'You do.'

'Right now, no, I don't.'

Alice leaned her head against Chrissy's arm. 'If you're good you might find something special after training. But,' she held up a finger, 'only if you're good.'

Chrissy was more than good, it was post-training and they were heading across the carpark, and still there was no card. It was making her feel extremely put out. Then Chrissy spotted something square and luminous trapped under her driver's side windscreen wiper and halted. She grinned, her blood pulsing with excitement, while her friends exchanged conspiratorial glances.

'It was there all along, wasn't it?' she said to Alice.

'It was.'

'Well,' said Paige, nudging her. 'Go open it. We're as invested in this as you now.'

She supposed they were, given Nick was using Alice as a conduit, which was why Chrissy didn't mind when they followed.

'Green glitter pen,' she said, showing off the front where Nick had written her name in his untidy boy's scrawl.

'Must have bought a variety pack,' said Paige.

Casting them each sly looks, Chrissy decided to give her friends a taste of their own medicine. She felt all over the envelope's surface. 'Same width as the last, I think.' Then she rattled it near her ear before holding it up. The centre's arc lights had been extinguished, but those over the carpark still glowed, and the moon was full and bright. 'Nope, can't see anything there.' She held the envelope to her nose, jerked it back and regarded it as though shocked. 'Do I detect ...'

'What?' said Alice, hands clapped together as she bounced from foot to foot. 'Has he sprayed it with something?' She turned to Paige. 'I don't remember smelling anything, do you?'

'I think,' said Paige dryly, 'she's teasing us.'

'Oh. That's mean.'

Chrissy laughed. 'Now you know how I felt.' She cracked open the seal and pulled out Nick's card.

Paige leaned forward. 'Is that?' She looked at Chrissy and across to Alice and down again.

Alice strained for a closer inspection and stared at

Chrissy, her mouth opening and closing like a goldfish before releasing a disbelieving, 'No-o-o.'

But Chrissy was clutching herself laughing. She dropped the envelope to her side and let out a guffaw before bringing it back into the light and laughing some more.

Nick had drawn a Friesian cow jumping over a moon. The moon was smiling. The cow was holding a rose clamped between its buck teeth. There were comets with glittery trails and bright-gold sticker stars with grins in their centres. There was even a spaceship spurting a multi-coloured jet blast.

Below, in green glitter pen he'd written: 'This is how I feel ...'

'Open it, open it,' demanded Alice.

Chrissy didn't need to though. She knew what would be on the inside and she was right. Scrawled across the centre of the card in more glitter pen was:

'... when I think of you.'

ELEVEN

CHRISSY EXPECTED another card on Saturday, but when she met Alice at the netball courts carpark her friend shook her head.

'Sorry,' said Alice, holding her palms open. 'I honestly haven't heard from him.'

'That's okay.'

Catching Chrissy's crestfallen expression, Alice put a hand on her shoulder. 'To be fair, they must take him ages and Nick has to work like the rest of us.'

'I know.'

Alice's eyes and mouth were soft with sympathy. 'You've really fallen for him, haven't you?'

Chrissy sighed. 'I don't know. He's making me want to though.'

'It's okay to fall in love, you know.'

'I know, but it's all so soon and he ...' She shook her head, frustrated. 'How is it he can see me now when he couldn't before?'

'We were different then, you've said that yourself. We

were young, made mistakes. It was *school*.' Alice gave a fake shudder, making Chrissy laugh.

'You're right.'

They walked on a little further. The sky was autumn clear. Long-legged girls of every age wearing bright lycra uniforms flitted this way and that across the carpark like tropical butterflies. Balls flew around them along with chatter and laughter. Alice and Chrissy smiled and waved at people they knew and kept an eye out for Paige as they manoeuvred through the bustle to the centre's main gate.

'You know your problem?' said Alice.

'No, but from the look on your face you're about to tell me.'

'You're scared.'

'Not that scared.'

Alice raised an eyebrow. 'He's not Owen. Nor is he the Nick you knew from school. He's a man now, a good man, who's clearly nuts about you. Chrissy,' she said, touching her arm and stopping their slow progress to the courts, 'the man made a cow-jumping-over-the-moon card for you, with glitter. Not only that, he performed a dumb wiggle-arse parade in the pub for you. He's doing his best to make up for ignoring you in school. It's time you stopped punishing him and gave him a chance.'

Which was what Chrissy was thinking about that night on the couch, when her phone lit up with an incoming text. At the sight of Nick's name, Chrissy's pulse took off like a thoroughbred from the barriers. It took two attempts to plug in the correct code to unlock her phone, her fingers were so clumsy.

Hey, babe. Did you win?

She smiled at the 'babe' and immediately texted back. *No, lost by 3 goals. You?*

Won by 16 points.

Well done.

It was my superior water-boy skills that did it.

Chrissy laughed, though she bet it pained him that his injury forced him into the lesser role of ferrying water to his teammates instead of helping them to victory on the field. *I'm sure.*

There was nothing after that for a minute or two. Chrissy supposed Nick was as tongue-tied as her. She was about to put the phone down when another message popped up.

Can I call you?

Her fingers hovered over the keyboard. This was the moment Alice meant, the time when she moved on and gave Nick a chance. It wasn't so easy though. For all their sentiment, the cards were playful and silly, a game they were playing. Phone calls were another level. Intimate.

I just want to hear your voice.

Chrissy blinked at the words, almost an echo of those she'd whispered to Nick the one time she'd spoken during her teenage mystery calls.

Okay.

It took seconds for him to phone. 'Hey,' he said, and Chrissy could hear the smile in his voice.

It put a smile in her own. 'Hey, you.'

'Not interrupting, am I?'

'No, I was just watching a movie.' Not quite the truth. She'd been so deep in thought she had no idea what the film was about. Chrissy picked up the remote and turned off the sound before snuggling into the corner of her lounge and closing her eyes. If she used her imagination, Nick could be here with her. 'I suppose you were doing the same?'

'Nah, Chops – that's my housemate – and his girlfriend, Stace, are in the lounge, stuck together like leeches, so I escaped to my room. Been lying here, thinking of you.'

Chrissy's voice was quiet. 'I was thinking of you, too.'

There was silence between them, as if neither knew how to respond to their admissions. Chrissy was the first to break it.

'No card today.'

Nick groaned and there was a rustling noise as he moved. She imagined him rolling over onto his side, muscular legs stretched out, facing his spare pillow like she was there with him. 'I meant to, but we had a few dramas at the farm on Friday night. Electric fence went bung and the heifers got into one of the new pastures. Had to round them up in the dark, then Dad tipped his quad bike and Mum had to take him to hospital.'

'Is he all right?'

'Yeah, busted wrist. Nothing serious. Mum's stroppy though. He broke the opposite one a couple of years ago, doing the same thing. Thought I might be able to get your card done Saturday morning and drop it by on my way to footy, but there was too much to do at home. Couldn't leave Mum with everything.'

'It's okay. I'll survive.'

'I'll have one for you Tuesday, I promise.'

'I'll look forward to it.'

They lapsed back into quiet. This time it was Nick who spoke first.

'I suppose I should let you go. You must be tired after netball.'

'A bit. And you'll be tired after everything with your dad and your water-boy efforts.'

He chuckled softly. 'Yeah, although my brother would

tell you that all I did was get in the way.' Another pause lingered. 'Chrissy?'

'Yes?'

'You really do make me feel like I could jump over the moon.'

———

By the time Tuesday netball training came around, Chrissy was about ready to jump over the moon herself, such were her nerves. As she'd known it would, the phone call had changed things. This was serious now and her crush, which she'd been forcing to stay dormant, had broken out of its chrysalis and was fluttering rampant wings throughout her chest whenever she thought of Nick.

'Gold writing,' said Alice, waving the card. 'This one has to be important.'

'We talked,' admitted Chrissy, 'on the phone on Saturday night.'

Alice held out the flat of her palm to Paige. 'Cough.'

Grumbling, Paige dug into her purse and slapped a five-dollar note into Alice's hand before scowling at Chrissy. 'You could have resisted a bit longer.'

'Sorry,' said Chrissy, not sounding remotely apologetic. 'Card?'

Alice handed it over, and Chrissy was grateful for the lack of mucking around. She might have had to resort to violence if Alice had tried one of her teases. After checking the writing on the front – neater, she thought, which reinforced her feeling that things had changed – she broke open the flap and lifted out the card.

It was the same thick stock he'd used for the others, except this time the front was blank.

She turned it over. So was the back.

'Wow,' said Paige. 'That's deep.'

Which was not the description Chrissy would have used. She swallowed and looked from Paige to Alice. If the outside was blank, what did that mean for the inside?

Alice had her palms joined prayer-like in front of her mouth. 'Please open it.'

Chrissy took a deep breath and did so.

'*All days are nights to see till I see thee,*
And nights bright days when dreams do show thee me.

By some bloke called Shakespeare, not me. But I know what he means because I think of you day and night. Every breath, every heartbeat.'

She passed it to Paige, who let Alice read over her shoulder. The pair looked up at her with eyes like headlight-startled rabbits.

'He quoted you Shakespeare,' said Alice breathlessly.

Chrissy curled her fist to her mouth and nodded, too emotional to speak. *Every breath, every heartbeat.* Oh, God. Any second she was going to float skywards, her heart was ballooning so big in her chest.

Paige, as always, recovered first. 'I tell you something.'

'What?' asked Alice.

She pointed at Chrissy. 'You'd better do something with that man soon because I swear, if you don't, I will.'

———

All Chrissy could think of to text Nick when she arrived home that night was *Thank you.*

He texted, *You're welcome, babe* straight back.

She thought about calling him, but what to say? That she thought she was in love with him? They hadn't even been on a date, hadn't kissed, hadn't done anything except exchange messages and share those fraught, close minutes in the Arms. Minutes where Nick had held her hand like it was precious and gently rubbed the back of her thumb with his. Followed by that insane, heat-filled moment when she'd stood on tip-toe, the length of her body pressed against his, and whispered that he had catching up to do.

Her phone lit up again.

Two to go.

Two? That wasn't right. Chrissy told Nick she'd given him five cards at school. Nick was up to four already.

Two?

Yeah.

?

You'll see.

'Oh,' she said, shaking the phone when no more messages appeared. 'That is so not fair.'

But Chrissy slipped into bed smiling anyway, wishing it was Thursday, and thinking of Nick and the most romantic words she'd ever read. And they weren't Shakespeare's.

Every breath, every heartbeat.

'Mine, too,' she whispered to the night.

TWELVE

NICK LOVED HIS FOOTY CLUB, he really did, but right now he was ready to tell the Mount Pitt seniors coach exactly where he could shove the football he was carrying. Nick would even help him do it.

Coach Stu gave the ball another twirl. 'Ten more minutes.'

'Seriously,' said Nick, 'I gotta go.'

Having arrived at training late from the farm, muddy and greasy, and headed straight out onto the field, Nick was now in desperate need of a shower. If Stu kept him any longer he wouldn't arrive back in Levenham in time to meet Chrissy at the netball courts. And he needed to meet her, otherwise he'd have to wait until Thursday to see her and he'd be crazy by then.

'We don't have hangers-on in our team, Burroughs. You don't train, you don't get picked.'

'What's up?' asked Danny, wandering over.

'I gotta get out of here.'

Coach Stu folded his arms. 'You know the rules.'

Danny cocked his head at Nick. 'What's the hurry? Ah,'

he said, then gripped Nick's shoulder and gave it a squeeze. They shared a look, one that came from deep brotherly love and understanding. Earlier in the year, Danny had been prepared to forfeit a cricket final to fight for Beth, although fortunately it hadn't come to that. The Burroughs boys were loyal to their teams, but when it came to the crunch, the people they loved mattered more. 'You know what's more important.'

'Yeah, I do.' Nick shrugged at Stu. 'Guess I'll be missing another week. See you.' And without a backward glance, he jogged towards the change rooms.

It was just as well, Nick mused as he drove into Levenham. He'd been hiding it, but he'd reinjured his shoulder lifting his dad's quad bike the previous Friday night and the rotten thing was giving him all sorts of grief. Impressed by his rapid recovery, the physio had granted him an early all-clear to play, which had cheered Nick up so much he forgot he still needed to take care. It was such a normal thing to do that Nick hadn't thought twice about righting the quad bike. Now the weakness was back whenever he stretched up his arms, along with more than a little discomfort.

Nick had kept his trap shut about it because he wanted to play footy. He'd also got himself so fit from all the running he'd done to make up for the drills he couldn't do, he was jumping out of his skin.

Then again, that could have just been Chrissy.

He was so gone on her, she had him quoting Shakespeare, of all things. Shakespeare! Nick hated Shakespeare. When he'd been made to study *Romeo and Juliet* at school, he'd been howled down for calling Romeo an idiot. But it was true. Romeo *was* an idiot. The bloke was meant to be in love with Rosaline and yet one look at Juliet and he's being led by his balls to her doorstep. That no one saw the problem with that still flummoxed him.

Chrissy had Nick by something bigger and more important than his balls, mind. His heart was so tight in her grip it'd never come free. He didn't want it to either. Which is why tonight was so important. Tonight was going to change everything.

He glanced at the envelope on the passenger seat. No glittery writing this time. No leaping cows, farting unicorns, butterflies or posies. And no Shakespeare quotes. Just his own words and not very good ones at that, but Nick meant every one of them.

'Just a bloke,' he murmured to himself, reciting the first bit of the inscription.

He hoped it was enough.

The arc lights over the netball courts were dying when he pulled into the carpark and for a horrible, chest-constricting moment Nick thought he was too late, but the clubroom lights were still on, and there were still cars in the carpark. One of them was Chrissy's.

He pulled in alongside and took a moment to compose himself. Then he shot Alice a brief text message, grabbed the envelope and headed to the back of his ute to wait. Nick leaned against the aluminium tray, tapping the card against his fist like he had done that first time, when he'd stood in a different carpark nervously waiting to hand over a different card, praying that the girl who received it would see it for what it was: an apology and an olive branch. Except this card was so much more than that. This card was a confession.

It was another couple of minutes before he spotted her. Chrissy was walking between Alice and Paige, chatting animatedly. Then she looked up and her step faltered. She stopped and stared, then glanced either side to her friends. Alice gripped her arm briefly before beckoning Paige. The pair walked away, leaving Chrissy alone.

As she passed him, Alice winked. Paige gave him a sneaky thumbs-up sign and cheeky grin that almost had him laughing. He focused back on Chrissy, watching her shadowed face as she approached, wishing for more light so he could read her expression.

'Hey,' she said, stopping in front of him.

'Hey,' he replied.

It seemed like all they could do was stare and breathe puffs of fog into the cold air.

The lights went off in the clubrooms. Three women walked out, pausing at the main gate to lock it, then heading off to their cars. Nick nodded at the one he knew, a friend of his mum's. The others looked at Chrissy curiously and turned away, smiling.

When the carpark was silent again, Nick held out his card.

'Hand-delivered,' said Chrissy. 'Must be serious.'

And from the way she said it, biting her lip after the first words, smile slightly wobbly after the last, Nick realised she was nervous, too.

He cupped her face, thumb stroking her soft cheek in reassurance. 'Just a card. You've had them from me before.'

It seemed to work, because she smiled. 'Just a card, huh?'

'Well,' he said, shrugging, 'it's from me so ... you know. There's going to be something pretty good inside.'

Special words for a special girl. At least, that's how he hoped she'd see them.

Chrissy traced her finger over the blank front. 'No glitter pen.'

'No.'

She turned the envelope over. 'Not sealed.'

'Didn't need to be. I like Alice, but curiosity can be hard to resist. I wanted you to be the first to read anything I wrote.'

'Probably wise in Alice's case. She's a terrible romantic.'

'Yeah, I got that impression.'

As much as he liked talking to her, all Nick wanted was for Chrissy to read the card, but she seemed reluctant and he didn't know why.

'I feel dumb,' she said.

'Why?'

'Because I'm nervous.'

'If it's any consolation, so am I.'

She regarded him with surprise. 'Really?'

'Really.'

'You don't look it.'

'Trust me, I am.' Nick tilted his head. 'What's wrong, babe?'

'I don't know. What if I don't react the way you hope? What if I somehow let you down or spoil things?'

He curled his hands over her shoulders. 'Chrissy, stop. You won't. I know you won't.' At least, he bloody hoped not. 'It'll be okay.'

She let out a breath and lowered her head to look at the envelope. When she raised it again, she was smiling. 'All right. But before I open it I want to say something.'

Nick felt her shoulders straighten under his hold. He lowered his hands to her wrists and held them there for a second before letting them drop. 'Go on.'

'I used to think the things I did for you at school were the most romantic things ever. I was wrong. Really wrong. What you've done ...' She was biting her lip, her gaze alight with admiration. 'Thank you.' She lifted her hand to her chest. 'Thank you for making me feel so wonderful.'

'No—' Nick cleared his throat and went to try again but stopped. Everything he wanted to say was already written on the card. 'Chrissy,' he said, touching her hand, 'just read the card.'

She laughed softly. 'Sorry. Okay, here goes.'

And with a tug the card was free.

Like the previous one, he'd left the front blank. Her fine brows furrowed slightly as she checked the front and back. Chrissy glanced up, and at his nod, took a breath and flipped the card open.

Nick watched her closely. Watched the way her eyes scanned back and forth, the way her lips parted, the way her hand fluttered to her throat, his own heart fluttering with it.

'Oh,' she said, except it sounded like a breath.

'It's true.'

She looked down again at the words he'd written.

'I'm just a bloke in love, asking for a chance with a girl he thinks is clever and interesting and gorgeous and sexy and nice, and makes his heart grow fat and beat faster whenever she's near.'

He moved closer to her and used a crooked finger to lift her chin until she was looking at him. 'Just a chance.'

She pressed her lips together, then opened her mouth, only to press it closed again and look back hard at the card.

Nick waited, electric with anticipation, and for a sickening second he truly believed she'd tell him no. Then she slowly raised her eyes.

'Okay.'

Nick smiled and Chrissy smiled back, and the next thing she was staring at his mouth and he was lowering his head and she was stretching up for him. His lips touched hers, carefully at first as he tuned in to her need, then stronger as her desire grew. The kiss was breathtaking, heart-thumping magic. The sort that made a bloke happy and fearful and lust-drunk, along with a thousand things in between, but most of all crazy in love.

He had a shitload more catching up to do than cards. He had however many years since school to make up for, and Nick was going to make every single one of them worthwhile. For them both.

THIRTEEN

IF THE WIND hadn't started lashing them with icy gusts Chrissy could have stayed all night in Nick's arms, but even his solidity wasn't enough to combat a southerly straight from the Southern Ocean when it blasted over Levenham.

He was, unequivocally, the best kisser she'd ever had the privilege to lock lips with. Generous, tender and breathtakingly sexy. Nick made everything tingle, from the tips of her toes to the tiny hairs on the back of her neck. As for what he did to other parts, it'd take more than a cold shower to get rid of that heat.

'You're shivering,' he said, nuzzling her jaw and working a series of kisses back to her mouth before finally pulling away. 'Time to get you out of this wind.'

Chrissy had the silly urge to mention that her bed was out of the wind but managed to restrain herself. Just. She really did want to go to bed with him, and from what she could feel from being pressed against him, she was in no doubt Nick felt the same.

He leaned his forehead against hers, eyes warm. 'I don't want to let you go.'

'I don't want to let you go either, but we can't stay here all night.'

'What do you want to do?' He grinned and wiggled his eyebrows. 'I know what I want to do.'

Chrissy toyed with the zip of his wool jumper. 'Tempting, but ...'

'Yeah, I know. Work tomorrow. Stuff it.' He sobered. 'What are you doing tomorrow night?'

'Nothing.' She took a breath. 'Nick, can we ...'

'Not rush?'

She nodded.

'Sure. Thursday night, then?' He kissed the shock off her mouth. 'I'm kidding, babe. Whatever you want. I'm not going anywhere. Friday good for you?'

Chrissy laughed.

'You have a great laugh.' He kissed her again. 'You have a great everything.'

'You don't know that yet.'

'Maybe not, but I'm going to make it my mission to find out. So, Friday?' He gazed at her hopefully.

'I can't. Sorry.' And she was sorry. When Nick looked at her like that Chrissy wanted to cancel everything for him. 'Alice is holding a girls'-night-in fundraiser at the netball club.'

'Shit. Saturday's stuffed because of footy.' He screwed up his nose. 'What about Sunday? I'll be spraying in the morning, if it's not too windy, but I can be free after that.'

'Okay. What were you thinking?'

Nick considered for a minute then smiled in a smug way that told her he'd come up with an idea and felt pretty damn pleased about it. 'How about I surprise you?'

Chrissy raised an eyebrow at him.

'Don't look at me like that. I've done okay so far.'

She laughed. 'Yes, I suppose you have. All right. Where should we meet and what time?'

'Uh-uh,' he said, shaking his head. 'First date. We don't meet anywhere. I pick you up and drop you home.' When she hesitated he went on. 'Just a normal date, nothing more.' Then he grinned and shrugged. 'Unless you find you can't resist my charms.'

That was the trouble. Chrissy wasn't sure she'd be able to, but what the hell. She was young, Nick was too, and he was handsome and funny and asking for a chance. Only an idiot would say no.

And if that meant they ended up in bed, well, it was hardly the end of the world. It might, in fact, be the beginning of a new one.

———

Chrissy waited nervously next to the brick mailbox at the front of her block of units. Nick was five minutes late, but he'd warned that he might be, depending on how things went at the farm. The weather had held and it was a glorious autumn day with only the faintest of breezes, the sky a cloudless and crystalline blue.

As he'd asked, she'd dressed in practical outdoor clothes – jeans and sturdy boots, along with a warm jumper and jacket. The smallest amount of makeup covered her face and she'd kept her jewellery to a pair of plain silver earrings and a watch.

She checked it again, only to look up at the sound of a car, and smile when she recognised Nick's ute.

He pulled over and immediately alighted, striding round the front of the car to gather her in a short but breathless kiss.

'You look perfect,' he said, taking her in. Then he swung one arm towards his car, bowed and opened the passenger door. 'Your carriage awaits, princess.'

'So, are you going to reveal where we're going?' asked Chrissy when she was strapped in and Nick had pulled out on to the road. During their phone calls and text messages Nick had refused to reveal his plans, but from the cooler and blanket she'd spotted strapped in the ute's tray, a picnic seemed the obvious explanation.

'Don't you like suspense?'

Chrissy rolled her eyes and pretended to ignore him, but kept casting sly looks across to the driver's side. Like her, Nick was dressed in casual clothes – a pair of worn jeans, leather boots and a fine navy wool jumper with a collar and buttons, and a chambray shirt beneath. The sleeves of the jumper were pushed up, the shirt cuffs rolled over the edges. He was clean-shaven and he'd had a haircut. Not much, just enough to give his habitual scruffy, straight-from-the-farm style a neater edge.

He looked country-boy gorgeous. Chrissy wanted to tear off his clothes.

'Enjoying a good perve?' he teased.

'I am, as a matter of fact.'

'Makes two of us, then.' He took his hand off the wheel to stroke her hair. 'Feels like it's been forever since I saw you.'

It had felt like that for Chrissy, too, but the anticipation had added to the excitement of today. Since Tuesday night they'd spoken daily on the phone. About silly stuff, mostly. Their days, funny things that had happened on the Burroughs farm, the raging wine snob Chrissy had served in the cellar door, Alice's hugely successful girls' night in, which had seen a lot of netballers rock up for their

Saturday games with sore heads and complaints of sabotage.

Last night they'd talked for so long Chrissy had been on the verge of asking Nick to come over and put them both out of their misery. But around eleven, when Nick had yawned and apologised for the second time in a row, she remembered he'd not only worked that morning before footy but was due back at the farm early on Sunday, and had ordered him to go to sleep.

Nick threaded through the back streets until he reached an intersection with the main highway. He indicated and shot Chrissy a wink, then turned and headed west out of town. Not far out of Levenham Nick took a turn to the right down a narrow bitumen lane. Within a few kilometres, they were deep into the lush beef and dairy country the district was famous for.

'Let me guess,' said Chrissy. 'You're taking me to see your farm.'

'Nope. Although we will drive past it.' He pointed to the side. 'That's one of Danny's windmills.'

There was pride in his voice. She inspected the shiny galvanised construction. Its blades were barely moving in the quiet air. In the distance, a trail of Friesians had their heads down in thick pasture, and though they were far from leaping, it made Chrissy think of Nick's card and smile.

'What?' asked Nick.

'Nothing. Just smiling.'

He glanced at her and reached across to squeeze her hand. 'That fence marks the start of our place.'

Like most of the other farms they'd passed, the Burroughs' was a carpet of green and brown, established pastures verdant with growth mixed with more recently sown paddocks.

'We produce silage, hay and beef mostly, but also contract rear heifers. Those ones you can see there belong to my Uncle Des. He still milks. Dad gave it up about fifteen or so years ago. Just as well. I don't think I could have stood being a dairy farmer. Chops loves it though, has milk in his veins instead of blood. You can't see it from here, but his dad's place is over the rise.'

'It's beautiful country.'

'Yeah, it is. Eighteen hundred acres of some of the richest land in the district. No vines though.'

'It's probably too fertile for vines.' At his frown, she explained. 'It tends to make them too vigorous. They end up putting all their energy into green growth when the aim is grape production. The rocky limestone soils to the south, like where Ryan's is, are better.'

'We have cousins with land like that, but they're diehard dairy. Don't drink wine either. You can help me educate them.' He winked then gestured to the outside. 'There's our gate and house. That fat thing in the front paddock is Ebony's spoiled-rotten pony, Hobbles. She's mad about that horse, but the rate Ebs is growing she'll be too big for it soon. Can you ride?'

Chrissy shook her head, her gaze still on the neat farm-house and its surrounding sheds. Shady trees covered a lot of the view, but from what she could see everything was tidy and well maintained. The entire property looked that way, from the fences to the pastures, to the fat stock. She wasn't surprised. From their phone conversations and how he spoke about the farm and his work, Nick loved what he did. She liked that about him, his passion and pride. Not enough people felt that way about their jobs.

'Word of warning for when you come visit, Ebs will probably offer to teach you. Whatever you do, don't say yes or you'll never escape. Look,' he said, pointing the other way. 'Mighty Mount Pitt.'

Chrissy laughed. 'Mighty' wasn't exactly the right description for Mount Pitt. Unlike Mount Stanislaus, Levenham's famous volcanic crater to the south and known to locals as Rocking Horse Hill, Mount Pitt wasn't much more than an eroded mound. But the flat plains around it gave it height and a certain majesty.

'Ever been up it?'

She shook her head. 'I've climbed Rocking Horse Hill a few times, but never Mount Pitt. Is that where we're going?'

'Yep. There's a spot I know.'

'Don't tell me, you take all your girls there.'

'It might surprise you that there haven't been that many.'

'Really,' she said dryly. It was hard to believe.

'Really.' He shrugged. 'Guess I've been waiting for the right one. Don't look now, but I might have found her.'

Chrissy rolled her eyes. 'You have all the lines.'

He laughed. 'When it comes to you I do. Except when I kiss you, then my mind kinda goes blank.'

There was a small carpark on the eastern side of Mount Pitt, with a walking track leading from it to the summit. A narrow bitumen road wound up the slope as well, but a locked gate blocked access.

'That's so technicians can get to the phone relay towers without having to cart all their gear,' Nick explained as he grabbed the cooler and rug from the back of the ute. 'The rest of us have to walk.' He took Chrissy's hand. 'Come on.'

Although not a hard climb, the slope still took effort. Chrissy's thighs were burning by the time she reached the top. Nick was so fit he was barely breathing fast.

She regarded him with mock sourness. 'You could at least sweat a little.'

'It's all the running I've been doing. This way.' Still holding her hand, he led her around the ridgeline to the southern side of the hill, where a rock formation created a natural hollow and viewing platform. Nick shook out the blanket and invited Chrissy to sit, before setting down the cooler and rummaging inside.

He held up a bottle of Ryan's sparkling wine. 'Apparently, this is a lively little number with fine bubbles, yeasty smells and a creamy texture. Highly recommended by their cellar expert.'

He set down the bottle and pulled out two plastic wine-glasses and, nestling beside Chrissy, popped the cork and poured them each a half-glass.

He pressed his glass against hers. 'To taking chances.'

Chrissy sipped and set the wine aside to take in the view. With the sun shining and the sky an endless blue, the breeze faint, and alone with a man who felt good and right, she felt blessed.

'Which is your place?' she asked.

Nick leaned in close and pointed so she could follow the line of his finger. 'That's ours.'

'It looks so pretty.'

'Not as pretty as you.'

She turned her face to give him a look and Nick took the opportunity to kiss her. A teasing peck at first, then his eyes darkened in response to her breathlessness and his mouth returned to hers and what was a tease became something far, far more intense. They eased down onto the blanket, Nick's hand cradling the back of her head, his body half leaned across hers. He tasted of wine and outdoors and sexy good things.

'Wow,' she said, when they finally came up for breath. Which wasn't too soon, the way their hands had been straying. 'Nice move.'

He rubbed his nose against hers. 'You wait, I've plenty more.' Then he closed his eyes and nuzzled her cheek. 'I am so crazy about you, I keep wanting to say dumb things.'

Chrissy's breath caught. 'Like what?'

She felt his smile against her skin, followed by a kiss. 'Nothing that can't wait. Hungry?'

Only for wild sex with him. 'A bit.'

He eased up and started pulling containers out of the cooler. 'Cold chicken. Lettuce. Potato salad.' He waggled his eyebrows. 'Dessert.'

'Dessert? And there I was thinking I was having you.'

That stopped his teasing. 'Babe, you can have me for entree, if you want.'

Chrissy looked at the sky, at the landscape, at her glass of hardly touched wine and back at Nick. What was the point in stuffing around? She wanted him, he wanted her. Taking things slow was all very well, but sometimes life needed to be dived into, head, heart and body first. 'Okay.'

His eyes went enormous. 'You sure?'

She nodded and leaned across to kiss him. 'Never been surer.'

'OKAY,' said Chrissy, curling up against Nick's broad chest and tugging gently on his chest hairs, 'we can do the getting-to-know-each-other bit now.'

They were in bed in her flat, where they'd been since their rapid descent from Mount Pitt and hurried drive back to Levenham. Such was their rush, their picnic food was still strapped to the back of Nick's ute. Chrissy supposed they should fetch it, but that would mean getting out of bed, and leaving Nick's warm body was the last thing she felt like doing.

Except for when he changed gears or needed both hands on the wheel, Nick had kept a tight hold of Chrissy's hand the entire drive. The moment she shut the flat door, he had her pressed against the back of it, kissing her so passionately her legs wobbled. By the time they made it to her bedroom, Nick was down to his jeans and Chrissy her bra. It was reckless and out of character, but not for one second did she question whether it was right. Something that felt this perfect had to be right.

Only when they were both on the bed had things

slowed, with Nick taking his time and in such a teasing way, Chrissy thought she'd combust from the desire he'd ignited.

He traced a circle over her shoulderblade with his finger. 'I thought we just did that.'

'That was knowing in the biblical sense.'

'I like this biblical sense thing. Can we do it again? I'm not sure I learned enough.'

Chrissy giggled. She'd been doing a lot of that. Giggling and gasping and moaning under Nick's sure touch. God, he was lovely. Lovely and sexy and generous and hungry, but in a good way that made her feel wanton and wanted.

More than wanted: loved.

'What do you want to know?' he asked.

'I don't know.' She propped up onto her elbows to look at him. 'Isn't that weird? There are so many things I want to know and now I don't know where to start.'

'Not weird. I feel the same, but I'm not worried. It'll come in time and I know all the important stuff anyway.'

'You do, huh?'

'I do.' He kissed her nose. 'I know you're gorgeous and smart, and,' he brushed fingers up and down her waist, 'you wriggle cutely when you're tickled.'

He grinned and rolled her onto her back, and holding her arms above her head, then began to kiss his way down from her mouth to her neck and chest, and sucked a nipple into his mouth. Chrissy gasped, her back arching into him. He released her nipple and blew on its puckered tip. When she looked down, his normally soft brown eyes were flashing with pure wickedness.

'I also know you make this awesome noise when you're turned on.'

'Really.'

'Really. In fact,' he said, keeping eye contact as he began

to move down her body, 'I think I'd quite like to hear it again. In the spirit of my biblical getting to know you.'

Which had Chrissy laughing for about two seconds before Nick had her making the awesome noise he so loved.

———

Paige narrowed her eyes at Chrissy. 'You're looking horribly satisfied.'

'That's because she has been satisfied,' said Alice, who was looking her usual cute self in a pair of hot-pink sports leggings and blue jacket, with a matching Alice band holding back her blonde hair. She shut the rear door of her car and faced them with a grin. 'Although clearly there's been nothing horrible about it.'

'Well,' said Paige, 'does he?'

Chrissy tried to keep her expression innocent, but it was hard when her thoughts were as far from innocent and they could get. She really needed to concentrate. The Rebels had a big match on Saturday and they were meant to be trying out new plays at training tonight. 'Does he what?'

'Kiss like Leah said. What else?'

'Of course he does,' said Alice. 'Just *look* at her.'

Paige narrowed her eyes. 'Hang on, you've done more than kiss, haven't you?'

'Omigod,' squealed Alice, pointing and hopping from foot to foot. 'She has too!'

Chrissy lifted her chin and gave a sniff. 'So what if I have?'

'Eeeee! I knew it.' Alice danced towards Paige with her palm out. 'Coughity-cough, loser.'

Paige threw Chrissy a mock look of disgust, dug into her purse and slapped a fiver onto Alice's palm.

'Taking bets on whether your friend has sex is not nice, you know.'

'Fun but,' said Alice, waving her winnings. 'Pub after training?'

'Sorry,' said Chrissy. 'I can't.'

'More sex with the stud muffin, I suppose,' said Paige.

Chrissy folded her arms. 'It's not all about sex, you know.'

'It would be for me, if I had your luck.'

Alice whacked Paige on the arm. 'Stop it. Can't you see she's in love?' She eyed Chrissy. 'You are, aren't you?'

Chrissy sighed and pushed hair from her face. 'I don't know. I think so. I want to be.'

'But?'

Paige shook her head. 'You either are or you aren't. There's no in between.'

'Okay, so I am. But you can't blame me for being careful. I thought Owen was a decent person, too, and he turned out to be a first-class shit.'

'Chrissy,' said Alice, 'I promise you, Nick Burroughs is not a shit. When I told him about Owen cheating—'

'You told him about Owen? When?'

At Chrissy's tone, Alice turned a bright shade of pink. 'The first night when he dropped off the card. I wanted to look out for you, that's all. Make sure it wasn't some silly game he was playing.'

'That was not for you to share.'

Alice wrung her hands in anguish, her words coming in a rush. 'I know and I'm sorry, but you had such a crush on him at school I knew you'd fall badly for him again and I didn't want to see you hurt. I'm sorry.' She bit her lip, and for an awful moment Chrissy thought her friend might cry. 'I really am, but I was truly just looking out for you.'

'I know, I know.' Chrissy sighed. She was lucky to have friends like Alice who cared, even if they did have big mouths. 'I guess in the whole scheme of things it doesn't matter.' She would have preferred he didn't know though. Having someone cheat on you was more than a bit humiliating. It was like being told in the most hurtful way that you were lacking something. Nick might begin to wonder what it was.

'More importantly,' said Paige, 'what did Nick say?'

Despite her annoyance, Chrissy wanted to hear the answer, too.

'Oh,' said Alice, recovering and giving a little joyful wiggle, 'it was the nicest thing. He got all angry on Chrissy's behalf and swore and then said that wasn't him, ever, and if you'd seen his face you'd know he meant it, too. It was very manly. I'd kill to have someone look that outraged on my behalf.' She turned to Chrissy. 'I think he really does love you.'

'How do you know it's not just lust?'

'Because,' said Paige, leading them towards the courts, 'lust doesn't quote Shakespeare. Speaking of which, you still haven't told us what was in that last card.'

'None of your business,' said Chrissy.

The nudge Alice gave her sent her stumbling sideways. 'Must have been *really* good, then.'

It was. Really good. *I'm just a bloke in love ...* Chrissy had been trying to believe those words since she'd read them.

'Good enough to make her sleep with him,' said Paige.

'No,' said Chrissy, jogging ahead of them and spinning around to laugh, 'it was feeling his other assets that did that.'

'Other—' Alice was too busy gaping to finish.

'Assets,' filled in Paige. Then she looked at Alice with a raised eyebrow.

'Assets,' repeated Alice, arching one of her own blonde brows.

'Was that a brag, dear Alice?'

'I do feel that it was, friend Paige.'

The pair began to shake their heads as though in sorrow.

Chrissy knew that exchange and what would come from it. 'Oh, no you don't.'

'Oh,' said Paige, 'but we must.'

'We really must,' agreed Alice.

'Hang on, you were the ones who told me I had to take one for the team!'

Her friends weren't listening. As they rushed towards her, Chrissy turned and bolted but was stymied by the sports centre's gate. Within seconds they were on her, drenching Chrissy with their squirty water bottles.

'I feel so much better now, don't you, Alice?' said Paige, standing back to admire her work.

'I do indeed,' said Alice. 'And I'm sure Chrissy does too. Poor thing was in danger of overheating.'

'You two,' said Chrissy, slicking wet hair off her face and pointing, 'will keep.'

Though she should have been cranky, Chrissy couldn't help the warm glow inside her. She'd thought it would take months to settle again after Owen and the move, but it was as though the moment she stepped back in Levenham the world had righted itself. She had a job she adored, was close to her family, had friends who loved her, and her teenage crush had declared he was crazy about her.

Yep, life couldn't get much better.

FIFTEEN

BEING GREETED at the door by a dripping wet Chrissy wearing nothing but a towel made Nick instantly forget his post-football-training starvation.

'Sorry,' she said, 'just out of the shower. Netball ran late.'

'Don't be.' He dumped the Thai takeaway he was carrying onto the table and tracked his gaze down her body, lingering at the edge of the towel, where a bead of water was sliding its way between her breasts. Dinner be damned, he needed to see where that water ended up. He smiled lazily. 'I like this look. Well,' he tucked his fingers inside the top of the towel, bowing his head towards hers, 'I'd like it more if this was gone.' And, distracting her with a kiss, Nick tugged and sent the towel to where it belonged, the floor.

Chrissy, naked. More than naked. Naked and hard-nippled and wet and keening that cute noise she made when she was really getting into his kisses. Jesus, he was nuts about her.

'Dinner,' she breathed as Nick steered her with more kisses towards her bedroom.

'Can wait. And you're much, much tastier.' Then he nibbled at her ear, making her squeal and squirm against him, and causing Nick's brain to temporarily relocate to his groin.

Afterwards, they ate reheated spring rolls and jungle curry and rice on their laps in front of the telly and nestled back to nurse their full bellies. Nick couldn't stop looking at Chrissy. He felt soppy and smug and scared all at once. She was everything he'd ever wanted in a girl, and it made him want to touch her all the time, to check that she was still with him, that he'd have a chance to catch her back and plead his case if he ever did something dumb enough to make her want to leave him.

Last night, after he'd spent an hour in his room stretched out on his bed with his eyes closed, talking to her about the dumb shit they managed to fill their conversations with – dumb shit that somehow meant the world and more – Nick had dug the last blank card out of its box and held it.

The previous week, when he'd teased her that there were two cards to go, he'd planned to make this one a simple 'I love you'. Now that didn't seem enough and he'd kind of already admitted it in the previous card with his 'just a bloke in love' inscription, and God knows he'd dropped enough hints since about how he felt.

The trouble was, he still wasn't sure about her feelings. She liked him, a lot. She laughed with him and looked at him with a smile in her eyes, and sex was pretty frigging mind-blowing. The love thing though was a bit of a mystery. Yeah, it was early days and she'd been hurt by her cheating shit ex, but when you loved, you loved. The only thing about time that mattered was how long your lives together would be.

Nick glanced at her again. She was wearing a long t-shirt that only just covered the edge of her knickers. Legs, that minutes before been wrapped around his hips, were now rested across his thighs. He ran his hand over her smooth shins and smiled at the way her painted toenails sparkled. He wondered if it was a deliberate choice, to match his work with the glitter pen.

'Chrissy ...'

'Mm?'

Her phone rang. Smiling an apology, Chrissy eased her legs off his and leaned across the coffee table to check the screen. She snatched up the phone and stood, pacing quickly away from the lounge.

'Chrissy James.' A pause, then Chrissy was reaching for the kitchen bench. 'Oh, God. Kai and the others? Are they ... Okay, okay.' She breathed hard, Nick watching with growing alarm. 'Yes. Uh-huh. I'll come now ... I know, but I want to. Ryan's matters to me, too, Shaun.'

Her hand fell to her side and for a moment all she did was stare towards her bedroom. Then she bolted.

'Chrissy?' Nick raced after her, leaping the couch like it wasn't there. He found her yanking on jeans and boots. She banged open a wardrobe door and snatched out a thick coat and dug her arms into the sleeves. 'What's happened?'

'It's Ryan's. There's a fire.' She stopped and swallowed, her skin pale with shock. 'It's bad.'

'I'll drive.'

'No, it's fine. You go home. I could be all night.'

'Chrissy,' he said, grabbing her hands and cradling them between his. They hadn't left the house and already she was shaking. 'You're my girl and you're upset. I'm not going anywhere unless it's with you.'

He held her hand for most of the drive. Other than saying everyone was all right, Chrissy didn't know many details. It was serious though. Nick could tell by the way she kept her face turned away and gnawed on her bottom lip.

'It'll be okay,' he said for about the fifth time and squeezed her hand, but Chrissy shook her head.

Despite the fire trucks and crews working flat out, the fire was strong enough that flames were erupting out of the restaurant windows when they arrived. Chrissy gave a strangled moan and pushed out of the ute before it came to a stop. She ran to a huddle of people watching the crews work. Nick recognised the profile of the big chef Kai. Chrissy shared an embrace with him before moving on to greet the others.

Nick walked over and introduced himself to the group, and spotted Shaun and Alistair Ryan talking to the Country Fire Service commander. Seeing Chrissy, Shaun broke away and strode across.

'The restaurant's gone,' he said, squinting back at the fire. 'They're hoping to save the warehouse, but it's not looking good.'

'The winery?' asked Chrissy.

'Should be okay.'

'Any idea how it started?' asked Nick.

Shaun shook his head. 'Investigators will sort that.' Suddenly he slumped and rubbed his face.

Nick gripped Shaun's shoulder and gave it a brief press. There wasn't much that could be said. All they could do was trust in the crews and hope for the best.

It took another half-hour before the commander declared the fire under control. By that point the restaurant roof had partially collapsed. The cellar door and Chrissy's office were gutted, and a good part of the warehouse had been damaged. How much stock had been lost wouldn't be known until daylight, assuming anyone was allowed inside to check.

Shaun urged his staff to go home. There was nothing that could be done and no need for them to stand all night in the cold. The restaurant staff and those patrons that had hung around to gawp at the action wandered off, but Chrissy and Kai seemed anchored. Kai had his arm around Chrissy, while she clung to his waist, her head pressed against his chest. The chef was openly crying. Chrissy looked shell-shocked. Nick tried not to feel disturbed that she'd turned elsewhere for comfort.

It was after midnight when the fire crews finally departed. Under the moonlight, with smoke drifting, the collapsed restaurant took on an unreal appearance, like a ghostly ruin. The Ryans' faces were ghostly, too, pale and grim, and Nick's heart went out to them. He offered his help, volunteering the Burroughs clan as well, knowing it was what his family would want and expect. They were country people who pulled together in times of crisis, and the Ryans were liked and respected.

'Come on,' said Nick to Chrissy. 'Let's get you home.'

For a moment he thought she'd insist on staying longer, but after a pause Chrissy allowed him to guide her to the car, only to halt at its bumper and turn shiny eyes to her devastated workplace. She looked sad and beautiful and fragile, and all Nick wanted to do was hold her protectively against him. He cupped her face instead. Her skin was cold.

'Please, baby. You need sleep. You'll be no good to the Ryans if you're dead on your feet.'

The ute's small interior was thick with Nick's worry and Chrissy's silence for the drive home. He kept glancing at her, wishing he knew what was going on in her head. She seemed so lost, with her knuckles pressed against her mouth and her stare unfocused, and it made him feel like he'd missed something, when he never wanted to miss anything to do with her.

'It'll be okay,' he said.

She dropped her fist and gave a tired, unhappy sigh, then she reached for his fingers and squeezed them. 'Let's hope you're right.'

———

Nick roused and frowned. He was dead tired, but something had woken him. He listened, hearing nothing at first, then he heard a quiet sob.

Immediately, he rolled onto his side and reached for Chrissy. She was huddled at the very edge of the bed, face turned into her pillow. Pale moonlight filtering through the blinds caught the line of her hunched body. The blankets trembled as she suppressed another sob.

'Chrissy, Chrissy, shh, shh,' he whispered, turning her into him and cradling her close. He kissed her hair and wet face. 'Don't cry, baby, please don't cry. It'll be okay, I promise.'

'It's not fair. They all love that place so much and now it's ruined.'

'Not all of it, and the Ryans aren't the kind of people to lay down and die. They'll rebuild. Something bigger and better, you'll see.'

'What if they can't? What if there's a problem with the insurance? What about poor Kai? The restaurant was his baby. He was so proud of it. Now what's he going to do?'

'Chrissy, honey, you're worrying about things that haven't happened and probably won't. I know it looks bad right now, but it'll work out. Everyone will pull together like they always do. Ryan's will be back on its feet in no time.'

She shook her head.

Nick held her tighter, confused by her pessimism. The Chrissy he knew was braver than this. 'What is it, babe? This isn't like you.' When she didn't answer, he used his finger to tilt her head up. Even in the dim light he could see how deep her anguish went. 'Talk to me. Let me make it better.'

'You can't.'

'Why not?'

In the night, her silence sounded loud.

'What, Chrissy?' He cradled his hands around her face and searched it for answers, but all he could see was despair. 'Please, baby. You're scaring me.'

She closed her eyes and breathed, then opened them again. 'This fire ... Nick, there's a real chance it might cost me my job.'

'Hey, none of that. You heard Shaun, the winery's safe. You'll be office-less for a while and probably have to work out of a shed, but that'll only be temporary. And you can operate a cellar door from elsewhere in the winery. As for the restaurant, that'll just take time.'

'You don't understand. It's not the office that's the problem, or the restaurant or cellar door.'

Another tear leaked from her eye, then another, her voice choking with them. Nick's stomach knotted. Something bad was coming, he could feel it. Something he wouldn't be able to fix with words or love.

'It's the warehouse. The wine stocks. If they're gone then chances are so am I. After all, what use is a marketing manager if there's nothing to sell?'

CHRISSY TURNED up to work the next morning, exhausted and fearful, only for the Ryans to tell her she had the day off. Until the site was deemed safe and assessed by the investigators, there was little she could do, and the Ryans wanted time to work out their next steps.

'Come out to the farm,' said Nick, when she phoned him. 'Mum's only met you the once at her party and she's dying for a proper chat. I can give you a tour, show you what I get up to all day, besides daydream about you.'

What Chrissy really wanted was sleep, but the way her mind was racing she doubted that'd be possible. She could do with some comforting too. Despite Nick's assurances, that the Ryans were making decisions without her input didn't sound promising to Chrissy.

Nick was in the yard when she arrived, a black-and-tan kelpie at his feet. As soon as Chrissy was out of the car he was holding her. Not saying anything, just wrapping her close against his solid body, sharing his strength.

He eased back and cupped her face. 'How's my girl?'

'Tired.'

'Me, too. I've already told Dad I'm knocking off after lunch. I'll grab some stuff in town then we'll nap this arvo and tonight I'll cook us a casserole.'

'A casserole?'

'Yeah. Mum's recipe for lamb shanks. You'll love it.' He took her hand. 'You're just in time for morning tea. Mum's made date-and-walnut loaf.'

Any other day and Chrissy would be nervous about formally meeting Nick's parents, but she was too weary and upset about the Ryans, and worried about her job to expend the energy on nerves. They were as lovely as they'd been at the party, when she'd served them. Judy took one look at Chrissy and immediately started fussing mumsily, pushing her into a chair and pouring tea and shoving a thick slice of cake Chrissy's way, while Steve impressed her with his concern over the Ryans.

'You'll have your work cut out, too, I imagine,' he said. 'With the warehouse out of action, that'll affect orders.'

'Yes,' said Chrissy. She'd mentioned the same to Shaun, wanting to contact customers immediately, but he said he'd take care of it. Which left her feeling even more anxious. Customer service was her job. 'Assuming we have stock left to deliver.'

'When will you know?'

'I'm not sure. Shaun said they're sending people from Adelaide for the investigation.'

'I'm sure it'll be done quickly,' said Judy, patting her hand.

Chrissy hoped so, too. The uncertainty was torturous enough without having it drawn out.

Nick tried his best to distract her with his farm tour, but Chrissy's spirits remained low, and after Judy's comfort-food lunch of pumpkin soup and toast, Nick told his dad he was taking off to look after Chrissy. When she protested, citing Steve's broken wrist and Nick's responsibilities, both Judy and Steve told her not to be so silly. They'd be fine. She needed their son and that was that.

'Your parents are sweethearts,' said Chrissy as she lay on Nick's bed with him spooned around her.

'Yeah, they're pretty cool.' He kissed the back of her hair. 'Now shh. Sleep time.'

Chrissy was trying, but her body was a bundle of anxiety. She rolled over to press her face against Nick's chest. 'I'm scared.'

'Don't be. I'm here.' He gently tilted her face up to his and smiled. 'Whatever happens, I'll take care of you.'

'Make me your kept woman, huh?'

'If that's what it takes.' He nuzzled her cheek. 'Keeping you. I like the sound of that.'

Chrissy liked the sound of it, too, but only in the emotional sense. She hadn't put all this effort into building her career to let it go now. Nick needed to understand that. 'If I lose this job ...'

'You won't, and even if you do you'll get another.' He kissed her nose, confident he was right. 'Clever and experienced girl like you? You'd have wineries pounding on your door.'

'If only it were that simple.'

'Why wouldn't it be?'

'Because there's no other winery like Ryan's around here.' At his frown of incomprehension, she explained. 'The others are all small, family-owned places. Nothing like Ryan's in scale. They're not even close to the stage where they need someone like me, or be able to pay more than cellar-staff rates. If I want to stay in the industry and have a decent career – which I do – I'd have to move back to one of the established areas like the Barossa Valley or McLaren Vale. Or interstate.'

'But they're miles away.'

'I know.'

'But that would mean—' He eased slightly away from her, gaze darting over her face. Nick's lips parted as though he was about to speak, then closed again as a deep furrow appeared between his brows. 'You'd leave Levenham?'

She heard his unspoken 'and me' and wanted to cry. The thought she might have to choose between Nick and her career had been tearing her up inside since the night of the fire. It was such an impossible choice, yet as much as her heart told her she could never give him up, her head said otherwise. Chrissy needed her career, it was who she was, and without it she'd be miserable. Yes, she could stay, and perhaps she might be happy for a while – who wouldn't be, wrapped in Nick's affection? Eventually though, resentment would grow and it would pull them apart in a way that could never be repaired. At least if she moved they might have a chance.

Chrissy nodded, her throat aching. 'I'm sorry.'

Nick rolled onto his back and stared at the ceiling, then suddenly he was holding her again. 'It won't come to that.' He was trying to sound positive, but she could hear the fear in his voice. 'The Ryans will rebuild. You'll be fine. We'll be fine.'

'It might not be.'

'It will. They need you, Chrissy. More than that, I need you.' He gave a half-laugh and pressed his forehead against hers. 'Now I know how Danny felt with Beth.'

'How was that?'

'Shit-scared.' One corner of his mouth twisted into a

wry smile. 'Seems like love likes to toy with us Burroughs boys.'

'Love?'

'Yeah, love.' His beautiful velvet-brown gaze softened. 'I love you, Chrissy. Have done since that first night in the carpark. And that's why we're going to be okay.'

'How can you be so sure?'

He shrugged. 'Because it's meant to be.'

————

An afternoon and evening of being indulged by Nick along with plenty of sleep left Chrissy feeling more optimistic. She arrived at work on Thursday to find Shaun in the winery with several open bottles lined up on a table and a glass in his hand.

'From the warehouse?' asked Chrissy, inspecting the labels.

'From the back bay. Museum stock. The rest is gone.' He swirled wine around his mouth and squirted the liquid into the plastic bowl he was using as a makeshift spittoon. 'Cooked. Every one of them.'

Chrissy fetched a glass and went through her own tasting. The colours varied, from normal deep burgundy to brick brown, and while some were worse than others, each sample had the distinctive stewed taste of heat-affected wine.

She studied Shaun as she tasted, checking his expression for guilt that he might have to let her go. He looked tired and sombre, which was to be expected, but otherwise his attitude towards her seemed the same.

He caught her inspection and grimaced. 'It's going to be tough going for a while, but once we hear from the insurance people we'll be able to move forward. In the meantime, we'll just have to make do. Dad's hired a portable office. Should be here tomorrow. Technicians are booked to set up phones and internet on Monday.'

'The cellar door?'

'Closed until further notice.' He gazed around the shed, at the barrels on their metal racks, the fermentation tanks and stacks of plastic Macro Bins, set aside clean and ready for next year's vintage. 'Nothing to sell.'

'I'm so sorry, Shaun.'

'Thanks.' He looked at his glass and the line of wines and sighed. 'Guess I better hit the phones again. Mum's looking after the restaurant bookings, but I've still got the outstanding orders to finish.'

'Let me do that. You look as if you could do with a rest.' She smiled to soften her words. 'If you don't mind me saying.'

'It's all right. I need to keep busy anyway.' He set down his glass and went to walk off then stopped and ran his fingers roughly through his hair. 'Hell. Sorry, Chrissy. Not thinking straight. There's a spare laptop up at the house you can use. You can ...' He glanced around the winery again, his body slumping with weariness. 'I don't know. What do you suggest?'

Chrissy straightened her shoulders. This was what she was paid for. 'In crisis cases like this, it's all about communication, stating facts, scuttling rumour. You're doing the right thing with the personal calls to those with outstanding orders, but it's imperative we make some form of contact with all our customer base. A newsletter for our subscribers, a letter for retailers, another for the restaurant and bar trade. I'd also suggest ...'

Chrissy continued to outline ideas as they walked to the

house, gaining in confidence with every appreciative look Shaun tossed at her. By the time they reached the Ryan's kitchen, where Yvette had just made a pot of tea, Shaun was rubbing his hands together.

'Right, then,' he said. 'Better get to work.'

———

'Told you it'd be okay,' said Nick, when he called around that night after football training and Chrissy filled him in on her day.

'We're not out of the woods yet.' That she was making herself invaluable was important, but it didn't make the future any more certain. Until the current vintage's whites, presently undergoing aging, were bottled, the Ryan's had no stock. And no stock meant no cashflow. 'The reports are still to come and these are only short-term measures.'

'Hey.' Nick tipped her chin to kiss her. 'What did I tell you about things being meant to be?'

'I know.' She toyed with the buttons on his polo shirt. He smelled delicious, of soap and masculinity, of strength and possibility. 'I hope you weren't expecting anything special for dinner. I haven't had a chance to shop.' And her appetite had been barely existent these last couple of days.

A lazy smile spread across his face. 'You think I care about dinner when I have this to play with?'

In a flash Nick's hands were inside her shirt and he was tickling her belly, and Chrissy was squealing and giggling and squirming in his arms, her fears dissolving under the force of his love.

'Chrissy, Chrissy,' he whispered, nuzzling and kissing her neck, 'you're so soft and sweet I can't get enough of you.'

'I can't get enough of you either.' She closed her eyes at

the feel of his lips working their way back to her mouth, but instead of a long, lingering kiss, he scuttled more soft kisses across her cheek until his breath fanned her ear. The sound of it set electric jolts down her spine. She was going to melt if he didn't stop.

His hands crept up her belly to cup her breasts, his thumbs brushing the lace over her nipples. He stroked back and forth, his breathing coming faster as her nipples responded and pebbled. 'I've thought about this all day. Touching you. Tasting you.' He sucked on her earlobe. 'Loving you.'

His whispers sent the jolts haywire. Every centimetre of skin tightened and puckered. Chrissy arched her back against the exquisite feeling.

Slowly, Nick kissed his way back to her mouth, lips and thumbs working their magic. 'I love you so much.'

'I love you, too.'

He lifted his head to look at her. 'You do?'

'Yes.' Chrissy bit her lip. She hadn't meant to say it. It was the truth though. She did love him. Madly, and against her better judgement. If things did go pear-shaped with Ryan's, she'd be facing a world of hurt. But somehow, with Nick in her corner, it didn't seem so bad.

He grinned, then he lifted her off the ground and hitched her legs around his waist. He spun her and let out a whoop. 'My girl. My gorgeous, clever Chrissy-girl.'

'Nick,' she said, when he kept spinning. His erection was hard against her crotch and the pressure of it was doing crazy things to her girl bits.

'Yeah?'

'Take me to bed.'

His grin broadened. 'Whatever you say, babe. Whatever you say.'

SEVENTEEN

IT WAS Saturday night at the Arms and the pub was buzzing with people celebrating sports victories, drowning their sorrows, or simply out for a meal. Nick was watching Chrissy with Alice, Paige, Beth and Harry Argyle's pretty beautician girlfriend, Summer. The group were at a table in the corner, planning more fundraising projects for Alice's assault on the Show Queen title, and although Beth and Summer were newcomers to Levenham, the girls were laughing and scheming like they'd been friends for years.

Sensing his stare, Chrissy looked up and smiled, causing Nick's heart to do a slow somersault. He winked, and grinned when she gave a funny little wriggle. Catching the action, Paige shot him a warning glare. Nick had been ordered on arrival to control himself and not to distract Chrissy. He threw Paige an extra wink to annoy her and laughed as she eye-rolled, then surreptitiously scratched her nose with an extended middle finger.

Paige could sledge all she liked, Nick didn't care. Chrissy loved him. She'd said it and shown it, and Nick had been walking on air ever since. The clichés went on: he whistled while he worked, grinned stupidly whenever anyone asked about her, spent half his day staring into space, lost in thoughts of her, and barely minded when his brother called him Numbnuts.

The only time he'd got cranky was when Chops asked him for a hand with milking while his dad was getting a skin cancer cut out of his leg, and a bad-tempered Friesian caught him with a headbutt to the ribs. Even then Nick could see the bright side – at least it wasn't his shoulder.

'You're sickening, you know that?' said Danny as he pushed a beer across the bar at him.

'Pot calling kettle,' Nick replied, turning away from the girls and raising his beer to his brother before taking a long draught. That afternoon he'd played his first full game of footy since dislocating his shoulder, and his body ached from the effects. If it weren't for Chrissy's girl session, he'd be at his place or hers, racked out on the lounge and resting, but these days wherever Chrissy went Nick wanted to be there, too. He had a heart on a rubber band, and it was attached to hers.

'How's house hunting going?' There'd been no time at footy to chat properly with his brother, and when they had it'd been about the game.

'Not great. Either overpriced or not what we're after.' Danny glanced at Beth. 'Beth's been fantastic though, getting the inside info on places. The stuff the real estate agents never mention. What about you? Any news on the Ryan's plans?'

'Not yet.' It'd been more than two weeks since the fire and the Ryans were keeping close-lipped. 'They reckon next week it'll be sorted.'

'Taking a while.'

'Yeah.' And the longer it took, the more Chrissy fretted. She was doing her best to keep her worry hidden, but Nick caught her restlessness and mumbles during the night, and the hollow stare she'd sometimes get when she thought he wasn't watching.

Danny went off to serve. When he returned several minutes later he leaned across the bar and dropped his voice. 'Listen, Barry let slip that he saw that chef in here yesterday and it wasn't for a drink.'

'You think he's looking for a job?'

Danny shrugged. 'Dunno.'

Nick stared at Chrissy. If Kai was job hunting, perhaps he knew something that Chrissy didn't. Like that the Ryans had no intention of rebuilding the restaurant. No restaurant meant one less thing for Chrissy to market.

'Shit,' he said. Then he looked at his brother. 'Give me a straight answer?'

'Sure.'

'How much of a peanut would I be if I had a chat to Shaun?'

Danny glanced at Chrissy and back to Nick. 'A pretty big one. I know you love her, but it's not your fight.'

'Everything to do with her is my fight.'

This time when Danny looked at the girls he only had eyes for Beth. 'Yeah. I know what you mean. Doesn't make what you're suggesting smart though,' he said, gaze returning to his brother. 'Take my advice, don't do it. Chrissy's a clever, independent woman. She won't thank you for interfering. She'd be more likely to dump you for it. Don't believe me, ask Beth or Mum.'

That Danny was right didn't make it any easier to stand on the sidelines while the girl Nick loved worried herself sick. What made it worse was that her anguish was partly his fault. If he hadn't pursued Chrissy until she fell in love with him it wouldn't matter. She'd be free to move on to another job, nothing risked, nothing broken. Now both their hearts were at stake. Not just hearts, but futures. Happy futures with a wedding and kids and thousands of special, beautiful moments of the kind his parents shared and Nick had always imagined he'd have for himself.

'This is fucked,' he said, staring into his beer.

Danny patted his head. 'Cheer up, Numbnuts. Things have a way of working out in the end.'

As Danny wandered off, Nick swivelled round to watch Chrissy and was once more rewarded with a smile, followed by a cute 'oops' look when she was caught by Paige. The sight of her gorgeous silliness made his heart skip several beats before it loosened from his chest to go floating somewhere up near the ceiling.

Yep, it was official. He was a goner. This was forever love.

Now all Nick could do was pray that his brother was right.

———

Nick glanced at the kitchen clock again. Chrissy had texted late that afternoon to say she'd be calling around to her parents' place after work and was likely to be waylaid, but she should have been here by now.

He'd asked Chops to make himself scarce and his house-mate had obliged by staying overnight at the farm. If she didn't arrive soon, they'd have no playtime before bed and Nick had fun plans for their evening alone. Plans that included a bath bomb and squeaky rubber duck for the house's big old tub. Daft yeah, but kind of funny, too. Anything to help cheer Chrissy up. And himself.

God knows, they both needed it. Danny's gossip about Kai had knocked Nick's confidence that everything would somehow work out okay. That Chrissy's spirits remained low didn't help either. Saturday she'd managed to set her worries aside and enjoy herself, but by Sunday morning the bright-eyed giggly girl of the night before was gone.

Being Chrissy she hid her despair behind a positive mask, and if Nick wasn't becoming so attune to her moods and expressions she might have got away with the cover-up. He knew though, and loved her even more for trying to protect him, while doing everything he could think of to keep her flagging hope and happiness alive.

Nick gave his simmering pasta sauce another stir and rechecked his phone. Still nothing. He jiggled it in his hand, debating whether to send a text, and had his dilemma resolved when he heard a car pull into the drive.

He tossed the phone back on the table and strode for the door. Fixing a grin, Nick flung it wide and opened his arms, then dropped them when he saw that Chrissy was still in the car. The engine was off, but she was staring straight ahead, her hands wrapped around the wheel. Though the light from the open door must have alerted her that he'd come out, she didn't seem to notice.

Nick waited for her to glance his way and smile, eager to repeat his arm-opening routine. Meeting Chrissy after a period apart was one of his favourite things. So was waking up alongside her. Kissing her. Making love. Listening to her talk. Hearing her laugh. Watching her smile. Everything.

The cooling engine ticked. Cold seeped through his socks. Night closed.

The back of Nick's neck began to prickle.

He breathed out when she finally pushed open the car door. The interior light illuminated her face, and for a moment her expression showed only bleakness, then it softened the way it always did when she looked at him and Nick's frozen heart lurched into action again. Fixing a smile, he padded to the car, dragged her into his arms and held her tight.

'How's my girl?'

'I've had better days.' When he leaned back to check her face she shook her head. 'Let's get out of the cold first.'

Nick kept his arm around her as he led her inside, everything within him churning horribly. He hadn't missed that glimpse of down-turned mouth or the red rims around her eyes, but a biting Levenham night wasn't the place to learn bad news. Nowhere was, but at least the kitchen was warm and bright.

'Something smells good,' she said.

'Spag bol. Hungry? I can have dinner ready in the time it takes to cook the pasta.'

'Not really. Maybe a glass of wine?'

'Anything, babe,' he said, kissing her lightly. 'Which one?'

'The cabernet. How was your day?'

'Same as usual. I'm more interested in yours.'

He plucked a Ryan's cabernet sauvignon off the rack and grabbed a couple of glasses from the cupboard, watching her the whole time. The kitchen's fluorescent light made her reddened eyes worse, and highlighted the charcoal smudges beneath them. She caught his examination and attempted a feeble smile, but it was made with the saddest mouth in the world.

He set the glasses and bottle on the table without pour

ing. He didn't trust himself. The room suddenly felt too warped, his pulse too fast.

'How—' Nick cleared his throat. 'How bad is it?'

'As bad as it gets.'

Nick wrapped his hands around the back of a chair to keep himself stable. The worst was happening, and though he'd promised himself that he'd handle it, the reality of it was knocking the breath from his lungs.

'They're letting you go?'

She sucked hard on her bottom lip and nodded. 'Alistair and Shaun called me in for a meeting this afternoon. They were very apologetic, but in the circumstances ...' She shrugged. 'They just can't make it work. They've promised good references at least.'

Nick couldn't believe Chrissy was being so calm about it. She'd lost her job, for fuck's sake. Her whole reason for being here.

'I'm so sorry, Nick. I'm trying to be brave, but I know what this means and ...' Her voice choked as her control broke apart. She turned away, hugging herself.

'What? No, Chrissy, no.' Nick rushed to hold her as the realisation that he'd been a selfish prick slammed into him. There he was thinking of himself when she was the one who was suffering. 'Shh, baby. Shh. You have nothing to be sorry about. None of this is your fault. None of it.'

He closed his eyes, his face buried in her hair, breathing the gorgeous scent of her, unable to let go for the dumb fear that it might be the last time he held her like this. He whispered promises he had no idea how to keep, soothing her with words and kisses and his embrace, while his own insides splintered with anguish.

'We'll work it out, baby. Together we can do anything.'

He was a Burroughs and he wasn't giving up. If Danny

could find a way with Beth, so could he with Chrissy. Anguish could go bloody jump.

She sniffed and gave a teary laugh. 'Even create miracles?'

'Ah, but we already have.' Nick smiled and kissed her. 'We're in love. Biggest miracle there is.'

EIGHTEEN

CHRISSY DIDN'T BLAME the Ryans for her situation.
The cause was a random electrical fault that triggered a fire
in the worst place possible – a seldom-used office where no
one was aware the blaze had begun until it was too late.
Had it been the kitchen or reception or the bar or even the
main office, Kai or another staff member might have spotted
it and acted. None of this stopped her from feeling resentful
though.

It hurt that they couldn't find a way to keep her on,
especially after her work in the weeks following the fire,
when Chrissy had more than proved her value in helping to
manage the crisis. It hurt even more to discover that Kai had
been advised the previous week that any rebuild would take
a year at least, and that the Ryans were reassessing their
entire business plan. Instead of a cellar door and restaurant,
Shaun wanted to explore the viability of a larger venue,
with a separate space for receptions, conventions and other
entertainment. The local wine industry was forecast to
more than treble in the next ten years, attracting tourists

and investment, and the business needed to look to the future.

Chrissy pointed out that if that was the case they'd need all her expertise and then some. Not only that, the current vintage's whites were aging as they spoke and would require marketing, as would any wines coming to the end of barrel maturation. Now was also an excellent time to rebrand, create a fresh new look out of the ashes, so to speak.

Shaun agreed. Alistair did too, but to a limit. He was a conservative man and with sales curtailed, cashflow was a major concern. Instinct warned him to consolidate, see how the rest of the year panned out, and plan appropriately. Unfortunately, that didn't leave the finances for Chrissy.

Shaun had walked her to her car afterwards. 'For what it's worth, I think he's wrong. I think Ryan's Winery needs you now more than ever, but with Mum siding with Dad I'm outvoted. I'm sorry.'

'Thanks.'

'Any idea what you'll do?'

'Take stock, I guess,' said Chrissy. 'Phone a few people. Start checking what's out there.' Figure out something with Nick that wouldn't result in them losing each other.

'I'll help all I can. References, introductions, whatever you need.'

She rubbed her mouth. Even though Chrissy had suspected today was coming and had been mentally preparing for it, she was finding it difficult to maintain a professional façade in the face of her job loss.

What made it harder was that, for a while, Chrissy truly had believed she had everything – a career to challenge and reward her, in a location she adored and where her family and friends were close, and a relationship so magical and strong it was like a dream come true. No, not *like* a dream come true. It *was* a dream come true.

Now she could lose the lot.

Except Chrissy was damned if she'd allow that to happen, not without a fight. What she'd found was too precious.

She dropped her hand and held it out. 'Thanks, Shaun. I'll be taking you up on that offer.'

He shook her hand warmly. 'Call any time.' Then he did something surprising and kissed her cheek. 'It was a pleasure to work with you. I hope we get the chance again.'

———

Telling her parents that she'd lost her job was awful, but it had nothing on facing Nick. Chrissy did her best to be stoic about the news and not make things worse by breaking down, but he was devastated anyway.

Devastated but also brave, loving and wonderful.

Leaving her in the kitchen with a glass of wine, Nick had disappeared with the bottle and his own glass. A few minutes later he'd returned, grabbed her hand and led her to the bathroom. The room was candlelit and steamy from hot water pouring into the tub, in which a jaunty rubber duck bobbed. The air had smelled of lemon balm, and music piped softly from a speaker dock.

Taking her wineglass and resting it beside the tub, he'd slowly undressed her, blessing each patch of exposed skin with soft kisses and smiles. When the bath was ready, Nick had climbed in and helped her to settle between his legs and lay her back against his chest. Then he'd used a soft sponge to wash her gently, all the time whispering promises and I-love-yous.

The warmth, perfumed air, music, wine and his tender hold helped ease the tension from Chrissy's body. She'd begun to believe that he was right. Maybe love was the biggest miracle. A miracle so powerful it could conquer anything.

Chrissy had woken the next day with renewed hope and determination. After seeing Nick off with a long, lingering kiss, she'd returned to her flat, set up her laptop and notepaper and, with a large mug of tea by her side, set to work. By lunchtime she'd nutted out a plan, and by five pm she'd scheduled appointments with the council's tourism officer, the chairperson of the Levenham Wine Show committee, the president of the Levenham and District Grapegrower's and Vigneron's Association, and four of the largest local vignerons. All of them had been interested in what she had to say, and every one said they'd heard excellent reports of her work with Ryan's Winery.

The odds that anything would come of her efforts were small, but she had to try.

———

'Any luck?' asked Nick after kissing Chrissy hello at the door to her flat. He smelled deliciously masculine, of farm and hard work and Nickness, and all Chrissy wanted to do was drag him to bed and bury herself in his comfort.

She shook her head instead, and wandered back to the kitchen and the dinner she was preparing, although God knows the last thing she felt like was food. Her belly was too bloated with disappointment.

Today's meeting with the chairperson of the Levenham Wine Show committee was worthwhile only for the enter-tainment value of meeting Audrey Wallace, elderly matriarch of Levenham's old-money rural aristocracy Wallace family, who'd invited herself along. The woman was in her eighties, but had arrived turned out to model perfection in a pair of black cigarette pants, a gold silk shirt, and a black wool cape fringed with a golden fox fur that looked suspiciously real.

They'd met late afternoon in a quiet corner of the Arms, where, after ordering a bottle of Ryan's pinot – which Chrissy suspected was a deliberate test of her mettle – Mrs Wallace proceeded to quiz Chrissy mercilessly about her knowledge of Levenham's wine industry, where she saw its future, and what role Chrissy might play in it. The chairperson barely had a say, and was rollercoastered flat by the force of Mrs Wallace's regal personality.

'I hear also,' Mrs Wallace had said in her distinctive cutglass voice, 'that you are rather close with one of the Burroughs boys. Nicholas, I believe.'

By this time, Chrissy had the old lady's measure. 'I am. However, I fail to see how that has any relevance.'

Audrey Wallace regarded her with cool blue eyes. 'Quite,' she said, before reaching for the bottle and pouring yet another glass. 'Thank you for your time, Christina, it's been enlightening.'

It was a clear dismissal. Though her own glass of wine remained untouched, she stood, shook hands with them both and departed with her shoulders squared and her head up. Another waste of time, but at least Chrissy had done her best and the Wallace family had connections everywhere. She had a feeling Mrs Wallace wouldn't forget her in a hurry either.

'Never mind,' said Nick, cuddling her from behind and trailing kisses along her neck. 'There's still tomorrow.'

Tomorrow morning she would meet the tourism officer

before heading out to chat to a vigneron. Her final two interviews. After that, the well would be dry.

Her head lowered at the thought. She wanted to stay in Levenham so badly it made her bones ache, but she wanted her career just as much. And she refused to be a leech on anyone, especially Nick.

'Hey,' he said, moving round to face her and tilting her chin up, his velvet-brown eyes full of tenderness. 'What did I say about miracles?'

'I know, I know.'

'You're clever and talented and smart and gorgeous, and I love you. We'll get through this.'

Chrissy could only pray he was right.

But the miracle didn't come. Not the next day, nor the day after.

When a week had slid by without any further response, or any other opportunities appearing, Chrissy said a mental apology to Nick, and emailed off her application for the brand manager's position in Victoria's Yarra Valley, which she'd seen advertised a few days before. It wasn't that far away, perhaps an hour's drive to Melbourne airport then another hour's flight to Levenham. Manageable for a once- or twice-a-month weekend visit.

Then she slumped back in her chair, covered her face and let the dam wall of will that had been holding back her tears collapse.

CHRISSY WAS PACKING books into a box when her mobile rang. Though she wouldn't be moving into her old room at her parents' until someone else took over the flat's lease, she wanted to be prepared. Applications for the Yarra job didn't close for another week, similarly with the two other positions she'd applied for, then there were interviews to get through, assuming she made it that far. With only a minimum payout from the Ryans and casual restaurant work to keep money coming in, things were tight.

She checked the number. Not one Chrissy recognised. After another long week without feedback, she'd all but given up on finding a position locally, yet that didn't stop her stomach tightening with anticipation every time her phone rang. Taking a few seconds to breathe herself calm, she answered.

'Chrissy James.'

'Chrissy, it's Digby Wallace-Jones. You met with my grandmother Audrey Wallace the other week.'

'Yes. Along with Sarah Nolan.'

'Who probably never got a word in edgeways, knowing

my gran. Look, I was wondering if you're free for a chat one day this week. Afternoons are better for me, but whatever suits.'

'This is about a position?'

'Potential position. We're still exploring funding options and it might not work out, but employing a Wine Tourism Officer is an idea the Grapegrower's and Vigneron's Association has been exploring for a while. I should warn you it'd only be part-time in the beginning, but if you're interested we'd appreciate the chance to chat.'

'I am. Would it be just you and Julian?' she asked, referring to the association's president, whom she'd already met, and wanting to clarify that the 'we' Digby referred to wasn't a full-blown panel, in which case she'd need more preparation and background information on everyone involved.

'Along with Mayor Barry McClintoff.' He paused. 'And my grandmother. Sorry about that, but she insists.'

Chrissy smiled. She imagined it would be very difficult for anyone to say no to Audrey Wallace. Digby, Julian, the mayor and Mrs Wallace. An interesting group, but one she could handle. And this was an opportunity she couldn't miss.

'That sounds fine to me. Should we say tomorrow afternoon, around two-thirty?'

———

'We'll have to advertise, of course,' said Julian Koch, leaning across the meeting-room table to address Chrissy. 'Go through proper processes, interview other suitable candidates.'

Audrey Wallace pursed her lips as though the idea were truly appalling.

'I wouldn't expect any less,' said Chrissy, trying not to laugh. Euphoric wasn't the word for how she felt. There was a long way to go yet, but the opportunity she'd been presented with took her breath away.

She glanced at the whiteboard on which Julian, Digby and Barry had outlined their proposal, between interruptions by Mrs Wallace. As Digby had warned, the position was part-time, three days a week. Not ideal, but she'd take it. Funding came from a combination of council grant, a marketing levy on the Levenham and District Grapegrower's and Vigneron's Association membership, and a stipend from the Wallace family's private foundation, and for a part-time position the salary was generous.

Chrissy was surprised by the Wallace Foundation's involvement, which was more known for supporting arts projects. But with Mrs Wallace having been instrumental in getting the wine show off the ground and Digby involved in the local industry through his vineyard Gratia, Chrissy supposed the family could justify its interest.

It was also a job in which she had scope to create her own opportunities. The better she promoted the area's industry, products and regional tourism, and developed events and activities to complement those goals, the more secure her position and the greater the chance of making it full-time. In many ways, it was no different to her position at Ryan's Winery, except she'd be marketing the entire assets of a wine region instead of a single label.

It was a challenge and not without risks, but to Chrissy it was golden.

'When do you expect to make a decision?' she asked.

Julian shot a look across the table and cleared his throat. 'Well, there's advertising time, interviews to conduct. I imagine five weeks at minimum.'

'Don't be ridiculous,' snapped Mrs Wallace. 'That's far too long. The wine show is only a few months away. Christina would need to start well before then.'

'Gran,' said Digby in a warning voice that was ignored.

'The foundation is funding the lion's share of Christina's position. I propose we dispense with all that nonsense and employ the girl.'

'Audrey,' said Barry McClintoff, 'you know it doesn't work like that.'

The old lady sniffed. 'More's the pity.' Then she slipped a sly look Chrissy's way, before going on in a more conciliatory tone. 'Advertise, if you must, but make the closing date for applications short and the interview schedule even shorter.'

'We have to have due process,' said Julian, but everyone at the table knew he was beaten, even Julian if his tone was anything to go by.

Chrissy let the argument flow between them while she stared again at the whiteboard and its position description and chain of reporting. The list of goals was long and varied. Some of it would be new territory for her, particularly on the tourism side, but the very idea that she could be responsible for marketing an entire wine region – a region she loved and believed in passionately – made her quiver with eagerness.

'Well,' said Mrs Wallace, standing, 'that settles it, then. I do believe it is time for an aperitif. Come along, Barry. You can escort me and Christina to the Arms.' She cocked her arm out for the mayor and beamed at Chrissy. 'Perhaps, you can invite that young man of yours down for a drink, too. I hear he's rather dishy. One does enjoy a good ogle. Keeps one young, you know.'

————

Chrissy was already awake when Nick rolled over to kiss her good morning. It was just gone six, but at ten am the Levenham and District Grapegrower's and Vigneron's Association would announce the successful candidate for their newly created position of Wine Tourism Officer. Chrissy was confident it was her, but it wouldn't be real until she had confirmation, and she still had a four-hour wait to go. Four hours of butterflies and lip-gnawing.

Nick snuggled up to wrap a muscled arm over her belly. 'How's my girl?'

'Nervous.'

'Why? Everyone knows you have it in the bag.'

'I wasn't the only candidate, you know.' At least two others had been interviewed that she knew of, although what their qualifications were, she couldn't discover. Even Audrey Wallace had played dumb, and she was Chrissy's biggest champion.

'Maybe not,' said Nick, wriggling his way half on top of her and nuzzling her neck, 'but the others won't even be close to being in your class.' He nibbled on her earlobe, making her giggle and squirm. 'Bet they're not as sexy either. God, I love it when you get excited like that.'

She raised an eyebrow at him, and chased her hands down to his hips and beneath. 'Who're you calling excited?'

Nick grinned. 'Can't blame me, waking up to you, all soft and warm and cuddly.'

'You forgot lovable.'

'Chrissy-baby, that's one thing I never forget. Now, about these nerves of yours. Just so happens I know a sure-fire way to get rid of them.'

'You do, huh?'

'Yeah.' He winked. 'Watch me prove it.'

He did and then some, and when they finally tumbled out of bed and into the shower, Chrissy's body tingling from his lovemaking, Chrissy had never seen a man so smug.

They both were – smug, hopeful, happy. The weight that had blighted them since the fire had lifted, banished thanks to a single meeting. A bright future beckoned and both were eager to get on with it. All that was left was the confirming phone call.

'You're going to be late for work,' Chrissy said as she leaned against the tiles to watch Nick soap himself. His skin was sleek with water. Foam caught in the dips and hollows his muscles made as he moved. Sexy stubble lined his jaw and his freshly shampooed hair was slicked back, showing off the handsome planes of his face.

'Not going.'

'Why not?'

He slid her a naughty look that shot straight to her groin. 'Might have some celebrating to do.'

'We can do that tonight.'

'We could do it this morning, too.' Nick wiggled his eyebrows.

Chrissy laughed. 'I thought we'd already done that.'

'Nah,' he said, hooking the bath sponge back on the tap, and sidling towards her to plant his hands on either side of her head, his gaze on her mouth. 'That was for nerves. Celebration sex is even better.'

'Is that a promise?'

'Everything is a promise for you,' he murmured, kissing her.

After breakfast, Chrissy killed time catching up with industry news on her computer, while Nick flicked back and forth through the *Levenham Leader* and generally fidgeted. Whether it was from nerves or being cooped up inside, Chrissy wasn't sure.

Her computer let out a ping, indicating a new email. She opened it and puffed air through her nose.

'What?' asked Nick, then came around to her side to read over shoulder, although given the way his hands immediately started roaming, the email was an excuse. He scanned the request for a video interview for the Yarra Valley position. 'Typical.'

'Mm,' said Chrissy, squirming as he traced soft kisses down the side of her neck. Her finger hovered on the 'delete' button before moving on. She might still need it yet.

Nick pulled away. 'Delete it.'

'I don't know.'

'Chrissy-baby, the job's yours. You're not going anywhere. Delete it.'

But at ten past ten the phone still hadn't rung. By ten-thirty Chrissy was feeling nauseous and Nick had succumbed to finger drums and clock watching. The deleted Yarra job was in her trash folder. With a feeling of defeat and heat prickling her eyes, she moved it back to her inbox and rose to make tea.

Nick followed and caught her in his arms, kissing her face and lips, and smiling encouragement. 'Miracles, baby.'

His optimism was sweet, but they'd need more than a miracle if this position fell through.

Chrissy was about to reply as much when her phone rang. She looked at Nick, who immediately released his hold. Nerves buzzing, she strode back to the table. Her heart stopped, then a grin broke through. With a flourish she pressed 'answer'.

'Chrissy James.'

'I do expect in the future,' said Audrey Wallace, 'that

you will include Wine Tourism Officer at the end of your greeting.'

Chrissy laughed and faced Nick. He stood in the centre of her kitchen statue-still, eyes wide and shiny with hope. 'I take it that's your way of offering me the job?'

'It is indeed. Now, shall we celebrate with a spot of lunch? I happen to hear that Restaurant Ten has a new executive chef who's rather good at pastries.'

After settling arrangements, Chrissy set down the phone and looked at Nick.

He stepped close. 'You got it?'

She bit her lip, suddenly weak with emotion and relief, then nodded and reached out her arms for him. He wrapped around her like a man who'd just been saved.

'Oh, baby, I'm so proud.' And from Nick's husky voice as he held her and whispered how much he loved her, he'd been weakened too.

But together they were strong. Strong enough to make miracles and dreams come true.

EPILOGUE

'WHOSE IDEA WAS THIS AGAIN?' complained Chrissy as she puffed alongside Nick up the trail leading to the summit of Mount Pitt.

'All mine,' said Nick, his grin broadening. He really should stop smiling before she guessed what he was up to, but it was hard when he was holding in a surprise as big as this one. 'Come on, fit girl like you? Should be easy.'

She threw him a withering look but kept at it.

To Nick's acute frustration, spring in Levenham had been slow coming. Every Sunday in October had been miserable with rain, which was great for the farm and district, but terrible for his plans. And they were important plans, the kind that made his heart thump painfully with excitement and fear. The moment the forecast was half-decent, he'd committed and began his preparations. Now, it was happening.

He gripped the insulated picnic bag he'd bought especially tighter. It was bloody heavy and not all because of the food and wine. Anticipation gave it extra weight. Inside was the last of his promised cards and it was the most special of the lot.

The thought of it made Nick swallow and glance across at Chrissy. Despite her complaint about the climb, she looked flushed and happy. His heart tumbled over at what was to come. She'd say yes, he was sure of it, but there was always that little touch of uncertainty. Some days he couldn't believe someone like her was in love with someone like him. She was amazing – gorgeous, funny and smart. Three months into her new job and everyone was talking about the incredible success Chrissy had made of it.

Thanks to her input, the Levenham Wine Show had proved a massive hit and was likely to be expanded to cover more days next year. The local wine region had been featured in several newspaper travel sections, promoted as an undiscovered gem, and better still, Chrissy had been promised her position would be made full-time in the new year. Even more satisfying – to Nick's mind, at least, Chrissy was too professional for that – Alistair Ryan had called to say he'd misjudged and would Chrissy be inter-ested in rejoining them. The answer was a polite but firm no.

'We made it,' said Chrissy, pumping her arms at the sky and twirling, and if Nick wasn't on a mission he would have kissed her until she was breathless for him rather than from the climb. Instead, her led her to his favourite spot. The place where she'd said yes to him the first time. Where he hoped she would again.

The view was glorious. The landscape a vast and changing ocean of green from all the pastures and crops. The air smelled fresh and earthy, of mown grass and the faint tang of dairy cattle. Sunrays caught the minerals in the eroded rocks edging the peak and made them sparkle, reminding Nick of the card he was bearing that had taken him three days, a bucketload of swearwords, and a heartful of love to make.

He spread out their rug and ordered Chrissy to sit.

She eyed his picnic bag. 'I hope this isn't going to turn out like the last time we were up here, all that food going to waste.'

Nick hoped so too. This lot had cost a small fortune, even with a hefty discount from Kai, who, thanks to Chrissy including him in many of her promotions, was thriving in his new restaurant and scoring better reviews than ever. The chef had created a selection of savoury and sweet morsels, all of which he promised were Chrissy's favourites.

'Your wine, madam,' said Nick, passing her a bottle of French champagne.

Chrissy checked the label and raised her eyebrows. 'Wow.'

'Only the best for my girl. I figured you'd be sick of Levenham sparkling.'

'Wash your mouth out. As the person responsible for promoting Levenham's excellent wines I will never be sick of them.' She grinned as she popped the cork. 'But you know what they say, a change is as good as a holiday.'

Nick set out their picnic as Chrissy poured, and settled to laze beside her.

He pressed the edge of his glass to hers. 'To more miracles.'

She smiled and held his gaze, her eyes the colour of the sky, her voice soft. 'You're my miracle.'

A statement that made Nick set his drink aside to spend the next five minutes kissing her silly.

'You do realise where this is going,' said Chrissy, when they came up for air.

Nick did, and as much as he adored making love with Chrissy, that wasn't where he wanted to go. Well, he did, but not until later. He adjusted his jeans and sat up to pull lids off containers in the hope that food might take his mind off his aching need, and back onto more important things, like the reason they were picnicking at the top of Mount Pitt.

'I recognise those tartlets! You asked Kai to make this?'

'Yep. He promised they were all your favourites.'

'They are.' She peeked inside another container and let out a gasp, then clutched it to her chest and drummed the back of her boots on the rock. 'Salted caramel macaroons. There is a god.'

Nick plucked the container from her arms and set it aside. 'Eat your healthy things first.'

'Spoilsport.' But she dug in anyway.

Conversation rambled as they ate. Nick did his best to sound focused and intelligent, but his mind was on the card and the best time to present it to her. Before dessert? After? When they were packing up and he could whip it out in a 'look what I discovered' type act?

'Is there any water?' asked Chrissy suddenly, and before he could stop her, she was rummaging in the bag. She stopped and frowned, then peered down.

Nick watched with his breath held.

Her expression changed as she recognised what she'd found. She looked at him with her lips slightly parted.

'Take it out,' he said. 'It's yours.'

She looked down again, one hand curled over her chest. Seconds passed before she pulled out the envelope, and to Nick it felt like time on pause. The envelope was in a zip-lock plastic bag to protect it from moisture, and fatter than the others; fat with love and his message.

Chrissy turned it over in her hands and regarded him again.

'I thought you'd forgotten.'

'I never forget anything to do with you. Open it.'

Time hitched again as she first removed the envelope from the plastic and checked it over, then slid her finger beneath the flap to expose the card's edge. A smile, like dawn, spread slowly across her face and lit her eyes. Nick's pulse ratcheted up another notch as she tugged out the card and began to laugh.

Dozens and dozens of tiny 'I-love-yous' written in different-coloured glitter pen covered the card's front and back. They'd taken forever to write, but each one had made him smile, knowing it would make her laugh and remember the other cards. It was what was hidden on the inside that caused him great frustration during the card's construction. Frustration mixed with twinges of anxiety.

Chrissy crawled on hands and knees to him with the crazily sparkling card locked between her knuckles, and kissed him. 'You're so silly.'

'Sexy though.'

'Sexy and silly. Thank you.'

He nodded at the card. 'You haven't opened it yet.'

She shifted onto her bum alongside him, and tucked her hair behind her ears. Her cheeks were a pretty shade of pink, her lips shiny and plump from their kiss. She held the card in her lap and stared at it, then she took a deep breath and eased it open.

Nick said a silent prayer that the thing would work properly.

It did. Just as in the internet tutorial, the card unfolded into a pop-up of two linked red hearts. Beneath, in plain blue pen, Nick had written, 'Marry Me?'

He breathed out only for his breath to snag when Chrissy gave a strange squeak.

For an excruciating moment she said nothing, her head so bowed her hair covered her face. He could see the card though, and it was trembling, and with each silent second his frozen lungs became more painful.

Then she looked up and there were tears in her eyes and she was smiling and his lungs expanded and his heart started and everything bolted back into action.

'Will you, Chrissy?'

She nodded with her lips rolled together, then she was reaching for him and kissing him and saying *yes, yes, yes* over and over and Nick was grinning and holding her like the precious, perfect thing she was.

He gazed at the sky with Chrissy in his arms and kissed her silky hair. 'Remember that first night at the Arms?'

'How could I forget?'

He smiled. That night was tattooed on his brain, too. 'Remember how I said I'd make it up to you for ignoring you at school?'

She lifted her head and tilted it slightly, a small line between her brows. 'I do.'

He gave a crooked smile. 'Just wondering how I did.'

For a moment she stared, then broke into sweet giggles, her eyes still limpid and bright with happy tears. 'You did just fine, Nick. Just fine indeed.'

'Chrissy?'

'Yes?'

'That "I do" line? Keep practising. I've got a feeling you're going to need it.'

Santa
AND THE SADDLER
CATHRYN
HEIN
A Levenham Love Story

Santa
AND THE SADDLER
CATHRYN HEIN

He's found the girl of his dreams, but she's just passing through. Can he turn fleeting Christmas magic into forever?

Windmill fabricator Danny Burroughs doesn't have time to wait in line at the local saddler—no matter how pretty the girl behind the counter—he's juggling two jobs as it is. But his little sister has her heart set on a unique piece of saddlery for Christmas and he can't let her down.

Expert saddler Beth Wells has no idea that when she comes to small town Levenham to look after her grandfather's shop she'll be swamped with customers. Overrun by day, Beth is forced to work late into the night on Christmas orders. The last thing she needs is another.

When super-cute Danny arrives at the saddlery after midnight wearing a Santa suit, a broad grin and pleading she make his sister's present, Beth makes a deal—she will take the order in exchange for Danny's help. Except this flirty Santa's idea of helping involves more than stacking shelves, and in the confines of the saddlery their smouldering attraction soon becomes a blaze. But no matter how hopelessly drawn she is, Beth has a job interstate and a mum who needs her. Anything more than friendship is pointless.

Will these two chance-met strangers find the courage to gamble on their love? Or will the girl Danny's been looking for all his life leave nothing behind but a sweet Christmas memory?

A Romance Writers of Australia 2017 Romantic Book of the Year finalist.

Order SANTA AND THE SADDLER in ebook or paperback from your favourite retailer today.

Thank you so much for reading *Chrissy and the Burroughs Boy*. I hope you enjoyed Chrissy's and Nick's journey to love and happiness. If you did, and you have a few moments, I'd be very grateful if you could leave a rating or few words in review to help others discover my books.

If you'd like to know when my next release comes available plus gain access to exclusive content, news and giveaways, please subscribe to my newsletter via my website.

More information about me and my books, including the inspiration behind *Chrissy and the Burroughs Boy*, along with plenty of other fun stuff, can be found at cathrynhein.com.

Web: cathrynhein.com
Facebook: facebook.com/cathrynhein
Twitter: @CathrynHein